BRIEFS

STORIES FOR THE PALM OF THE MIND

BRIEFS

STORIES FOR THE PALM OF THE MIND

JOHN EDGAR WIDEMAN

Lulu Press®
3101 Hillsborough St.
Raleigh, NC 27607-5436

Library of Congress Control Number: 2010902249

ISBN 978-0-557-31004-3

10 9 8 7 6 5 4 3 2 1

Design and cover photos by Caroline Okun

Versions of the following stories were previously published in Harper's Magazine: October 2008; and Conduit: February 2010: Rain, Divorce, AT&T, Thirteen, War Stories, Fat Liver, Home from College, Giblets, Automatic, Message, Northstar, Party, Haiku, Paris Morning, Passing On, Writing, Breath, Trouble, Genocide, One on One, Barry Bonds: Home Run King

Also available from Lulu.com

A Glance Away
The Lynchers
Hurry Home

Visit www.lulu.com/johnedgarwideman

Yasunari Kawabata's

Stories for the Palm of the Hand

encouraged these stories for the palm of the mind

Contents

Brief Note on the Title

In the paperback version of the office edition of the <u>American Heritage Dictionary</u> (3rd ed.) I use when I'm in France, on page 109 below the drawing of a bridled horse's head that illustrates the definition of <u>bridle</u> (-<u>n</u>. 1. the harness fitted about a horse' head, used to restrain or guide 2. a curb or check –<u>v</u>. 1. to put a bridle on 2. to control or restrain with or as if with a bridle. 3. to show anger) comes the word <u>brief</u> (-<u>adj</u>. 1. short in duration or extent. Succinct; concise –<u>n</u>. a short or condensed statement, esp. of a legal case or argument. 2. <u>briefs</u>—short, tight fitting under-pants -<u>v</u>. to give a briefing to). The word <u>briefcase</u> follows <u>brief</u> and is followed by <u>briefing</u> (<u>n</u>. 1. the act of giving or receiving precise preparatory instruction or information 2. the information itself) and in turn <u>briefing</u> is followed by <u>brier</u> (<u>n</u>. any of several prickly plants, etc.).

Given the definition of <u>brief</u> contextualized as it is in the above citations, the short stories constituting this volume and the volume itself are called <u>Briefs</u>, and this brief note, curiously, could serve as the first story of the collection.

Witness

Sitting here one night six floors up on my little balcony when I heard shots and saw them boys running. My eyes went straight to the lot beside Mason's bar and I saw something black not moving in the weeds and knew a body lying there and knew it was dead. A fifteen year old boy the papers said. Whole bunch of sirens and cops and spinning lights the night I'm talking about. I watched till after they rolled him away and then everything got quiet again as it ever gets round here so I'm sure the boy's people not out there that night. Didn't see them till next morning when I'm looking down at those weeds and a couple's coming slow on Frankstown with a girl by the hand, had to be the boy's baby sister. They pass terrible Mason's and stop right at the spot the boy died. Then they commence to swaying, bowing, hugging, waving their arms about. Forgive me, Jesus, but look like they grief dancing, like the sidewalk too cold or too hot they had to jump around not to burn up. How'd his people find the exact spot. Did they hear my old mind working to lead them, guide them along like I would if I could get up out this damn wheelchair and take them by the hand.

Rain

Never ending rain had seemed the truth forever until the day he'd been born and rain stopped the very next day and no rain since. No one he'd spoken to had much to say about rain. Nothing good to say. They were glad it was finished. Envied his freedom from what rain had imposed on their lives. Why was he so curious about something people assured him had been no fun. Worse than no fun. Some people would shake their heads to suggest he harbored an unhealthy obsession. Why this worrying after rain. If he had known rain, they said, if he'd been there, he'd shut up about rain, they warned or advised or teased or just turned away to end a conversation they could not stomach. None of them, not a single soul yet, understood his need to recover what he'd missed, rain falling for the final time the day he'd been born, the rain other people had forgotten or had no desire to recall and him with a million questions, a million dreams, tears once when he couldn't explain his yearning to the only person who had ever seemed really curious, but how could he describe to her something lost, and worse, lost irrevocably, before he had experienced it, how could he express his loss because what was rain, after all, what could he say except the next to nothing others had told him about rain that had never missed a day before he arrived and would start again he was sure (and this might be the unbearable part) the instant he left.

Quiet Car

I asked her once, nicely, quietly. Second time I'm so pissed I couldn't trust myself to speak, just sat and stewed. Third time I got up and stood over her seat. This is the Quiet car, I said. Absolutely no cell phones. What makes you think you're an exception. She said fuck off, asshole, and I grabbed her phone and stomped it.

What were you thinking, Tommy.

I wasn't thinking, I was mad.

Huh-uh. Crazy. A big black man snatching a white woman's phone. Did you forget we still lynch negroes in America.

C'mon. It wasn't about race. I admit I behaved badly, but the whole thing's kind of funny, too.

Hope you convince the judge it's funny. Here's funny. Me, blonde and white and female, schooling a grown-up black guy about race.

Out the window he reads Libations then Cochinna's and then another familiar sign he forgets as soon as he reads it. He's riding the same commuter train on which the crime had occurred. Same signs, same rules, same cheating. Same blood on everybody's hands. He remembers her visit, pale hair sliding across her face when she leaned down to the speaking grill below the square of soundproof glass that connected them. Her play on the words cell phone he seriously didn't appreciate. A giggle maybe, he couldn't hear. Wonders if he'll call her again.

Help

Today we are setting out for Darfur. We are armed with bandages, prayers, good intentions. It may be too late already. Already we are weeping inside. The news from Darfur all bad. So bad some of us turn back before we start. Rumors fly. Countless rapes. Row after row of unburied black bodies stinking to high heaven. We're receiving our last briefing before the plane. A very pretty volunteer next to me with velvety skin much darker than mine. Dark as I imagine burnt twists of flesh on bones bleaching in the desert sun. I wonder if the rumors are true. Her eyes won't return my gaze. Her hand stiff when I wrap mine around it for a freedom song.

Divorce

He is dressing for his grown-up daughter. How strange, he thinks, peering into his closet. To be picking this and discarding that as if he's going to a wedding or funeral. Since when (how long, how long) is meeting her an occasion. A date. The peacock dashiki to give her a laugh. The good suit to offend her. Bell bottom jeans she'll smirk at or worse, ignore. As if he can predict the consequences of his choices in her eyes. As if he knows what they'll talk about in the restaurant she's chosen. The waiter setting down a cup of coffee that rattles in its saucer, spotting the white blaze of tablecloth before they can even begin. Not the waiter's fault. Nobody's fault, really, that their table happens to be at the foot of a mountain range with jagged peaks looming above them, obdurate and unimpeachable as annular rings of a tree. The crack, the fissure begins under there, under the stony folds of mountains stacking up, stacking up. Too much weight, too many years. The earth shudders, dances the rug under the poor, pompadoured waiter's feet, *Sorry... sorry...* he faintly warbles, *...excuse me*, a canary dying of what's to come.

Home from College

She counts her mother's missing fingers. Two more gone to the disease. Wonders if the rumor reaching her at school of toes rotting inside those ratty bedroom slippers is true. When she's away and scared, she counts the missing parts of her mother and the count always equals one. One mother. She smiles and counts again. One. The magic answer calms her each time she figures out how many mothers she has left, just to be sure, just to make sure. One. One mother minus two fingers equals what. One. Take away ten toes. Still never equals less than one. Until a day no absent parts to count. No more lost fingers or toes. No sad little round pot belly looks like it's full to bursting, tiny as it is, because her mother, skinny like a string, keeps no food down. Nothing gone away to count. Just the pink, slinky robe that always reminds her of the silvery one she was never allowed to suck her thumb with the silky tail of sleeping on her mother's lap. No missing poke of knee or nipple under the pink robe draped flat over the couch arm next to the kitchen door, the couch end where her mother settles each morning. No new missing something to minus. Only a girl standing beside an empty couch who would if she could, subtract one from herself, count herself a missing part that starts the count again.

Giblets

Clara's dog Giblets had four legs. One leg for each day of the week. Now Clara Johnson understood as well as you understand that each week the Lord sends got seven days but Clara's memories are not your memories. Once upon a time, every Friday and Saturday and Sunday of every week were holy days in her mama's house and Clara'd get her ass tore up often and terribly, bloodied by any comb or switch or board or cord her mother could lay her hands on because Clara never could satisfy her mama by being as good as she was sposed to be from the hour they started till those three days of church and praying and singing and sitting still as stone were over. So as soon as Clara out on her own she amputated the merciless days. Her weeks four days long with no scars, no beatings, no screaming, no cringing in a dark corner. Go away, god-damn church and she never missed one of the cruel three days she cut out of her week, not once, never, just like Giblets after one long howl just laid there quiet and didn't miss his leg she chopped off when Tyrone from over at Mason's lounge told her a church he'd heard about commenced its holy days on Thursdays.

AT&T

They employ the same robot in prisons three thousand miles apart to inform you that you have a collect phone call from an inmate. Each time he wonders if part of the astronomical charge for a five minute call from a prison includes a bill for forty or so seconds of the lady robot's time announcing, interrupting, signing off. Once he'd responded to her, imitating her recorded voice, the robot cadence and tone she'd taught him. Proposed marriage. Why not. Two could live as comfortably as one on the enormous profits she must reap participating how many goddamn times a day coast to coast and everywhere in between in the misery of conversations between the incarcerated and those not. If you can get away with it, why not charge a rate fifty, a hundred times more than what the unincarcerated pay to speak to one another. Are you still there, darling, he'd asked her after he said, I love you and she didn't respond. Then he said, No... no, it's okay, you don't have to answer. You don't need to tell me your name and I won't tell you mine. After all, if we meet in the street, you, me, my brothers and sons and fathers when they're free, who'd want to remember all this.

Fat Liver

The campaign for attaining a higher level of enlightenment goes well. *Hurrah. Hurrah. No more foie gras.* A silly banner, she admits. And maybe a silly cause. Who gives a crap if it becomes a crime to force-feed ducks and geese, a crime to package and sell their agony, she asks herself. Imagines bloated black kids with tubes down their throats fed buckets of KFC, rivers of Orange Crush, tons of Big Macs. Imagines the iron maws of prisons pried open, dark bodies crammed in. Sees America's bare, fat ass upturned in the air, oil pumping in like an enema. Imagines her fellow citizen's fuzzy heads bobbing like baby birds in a nest, every beak propped open by a funnel, the grinning president stuffing them with lies, terror, disinformation, war. Maybe she'll skip the *foie gras* victory march and victory party this afternoon.

Ring. Ring. That must be Sarah calling. Or perhaps Samuel. Though a bit early for him. Either one, it will break her heart to answer. No, I'm staying home this afternoon. No, our chance for a life together is over. No. No. Please don't call me ever again. The disappointed faces of Sarah and Samuel blend. Separate tales for each one collapse into one long, sad story. Ring. Ring. She realizes she's crying and that her mouth's open. The phone with a million miles of AT&T cable spooled behind it pushing through her lips, filling her to bursting.

To Barry Bonds: Home Run King

When I was a young man, like you, I, too, experimented with anything I could lay my hands on to make me better at what I wanted to be. Like you—maybe—I feared only my color, my tainted blood and tainted, incriminating history, and occasionally late at night fretted over whether I could sustain the strength of will to save myself, but beyond these distractions, I really believed and told myself deep down inside that nothing could stop me. I'd get it done. Be a superstar beyond belief, in spite of or because of, any doubts I entertained. And accordingly allowed myself excesses. The right to hurt others. The right to damage myself. Woke up more than one morning in a puddle of piss, blood and snot and never gave a thought to turning around, going back home. Too much world to win and I was damned good at winning. People loved me for being very good and footed bills I couldn't have imagined once upon a time running up. Bills for things the poor boy I once was had never heard of. Things I didn't recognize till after they passed through my body and my shit stank differently. I became truly so good, so much better than the competition, I forgot anybody ever needed to pay. Least of all me. And let me tell you that standing here now swinging my bat as you must swing yours, at air, at mosquitoes, at slow, dreamy curve balls I whack but can't halt their flight and they splash gooey in my face, like you now, I'm half clown, half star, half martyr and half something else if that makes any sense, you know, or makes as much or little sense, anyway, as being called out if you swing and miss a ball three times.

Northstar

She said I find the idea of anal sex quite un-sexy, and he dropped the subject. A tube of lubricating cream that had appeared magically on the perforated seat of an antique, wire-legged stool which served as a bedside table disappeared. How come men think they can make up the rules to liberate women, she'd asked before the subject dropped. Two weeks later when it happens, on his knees hunched over her in the dark bedroom, he's alone. Alone as the last person alive on earth and wonders if that's how a fugitive slave might have felt the first night free racing through black forests and swamps following the Northstar and remembers a dinner party in her brother's garden, the moon and a solitary star shining high above the patio table where everybody's happy drinking and eating, then the two of them walking around a corner of the house, beyond the arc of light cast by a fat candle burning in a crystal globe on the tabletop, the sky full of stars, the quiet amazingly deep though they'd moved only a few steps from the others, and there he'd taken her hand and wanted to say, I'm sorry. I didn't mean to upset you. Just forget I ever brought up that business because it's not something that really matters, all that matters is how much we love each other, but he couldn't reassure her without bringing up the dropped subject, so didn't speak, and now on his knees, pressed against her in this even quieter darkness, gooey mess all over his hands, his presumptions melted, him too sloppy and droopy, alone, scared to move an inch forward or back, would she ever forgive him, would he ever forgive her.

Hunger

When my wish comes true, I'm milling about with a bunch of other academics in a huge penthouse suite, all of abrupt Houston at our feet through floor to ceiling windows, twilight a faint ochre glow silhouetting a fence of high-rises, regular and monotonous at the city's far edge where civilization terminates and howling, endless wild west plains begin.

My wish: another load of humungous shrimp delivered to the buffet table so I can grab more than I managed last time in the scuffle with my fellow scholars. On paper we all embrace logic, subtlety, discretion, but here we're ravenous, our cover blown by a tease of luxury many tiers above the level we've convinced ourselves a prudent person should settle for. No one I knew knew why we'd been summoned here. Or who summoned us. Invitations had appeared in our hotel mailboxes and bore no host's name. The weight of the paper, the gold embossed print dead giveaways of the sponsor's intent to impress. Given the prospect of good food, good drink, so what if our scruffy presence polishes a rogue corporation's image, who cares if some eccentric, drop-out billionaire gets a kick out of rewarding us or rubbing our learned noses in the fact of our relative squalor. The fresh mound of shrimp arrives, and in the scramble we would have trampled blind Homer, Shakespeare, Dante, T. S. Eliot, Jane Austen, Jesus, Buddha, our grandmothers.

After a thirty second melee of dueling toothpicks and fast chewing disappears every morsel, we slink off exhausted, dizzy with unquenched desire. Some sulk alone, others chatter in nervous groups, our eyes searching above our colleagues' heads for another flying saucer silver platter aloft on a liveried arm.

War Stories

I have a friend, a kind of friend, anyway, I talked with only once and that once we'd seemed simpatico. I let him know I had learned a lot from a story he'd written about things men carried when they fought in Vietnam. Years have passed and I've lost track of him, so to speak. I need to talk with him now because I'm trying to understand the war here in America, the worst war, in spite of mounting casualties in wars abroad, this war filling prisons, filling pockets, emptying schools, minds, hearts, a war keeping people locked down at home, no foreign nations to defeat, just ourselves defeated by fear of each other, a war incarcerating us all in killing fields where the only rule is feed on the bodies of fellow inmates or surely they will feed on yours. What do combatants carry in this war, I want to ask him, in this civil strife waged within stone walls, in glass cages, barbed wire enclosed ghettoes of poverty and wealth, behind the lines, between the lines. Can friend be distinguished from foe by what they carry, what they wear. By the way they walk, how they talk. Their words, their silence? This war different, though not entirely unlike others in Afghanistan, Iraq, and soon Iran or wherever else folly incites us to land our young men and women with whatever they will carry into battle this time and carry when they return like the chickens Malcolm warned always come home to roost. Not separate wars, really. No more separate than different colors of skin that provide logic and cover for war. No more separate than the color of my skin from yours, my friend, if we could meet again and talk about carrying the things we carry, about what torments me, an old man ashamed of this country I assume you still live in, too.

Segregation

Separate domains. Why would someone want to go where they're not wanted. Where they don't fit in. Where it's dangerous to go. *Why not*, asked the Grizzly Man, who trekked to Alaska to live with bears. *Why not*, asked the Austrian filmmaker, Werner Herzog, scavenging the eaten-alive, dead Grizzly Man's videotapes to construct a documentary starring him.

Who fits where. And how and why. And who says so. The primal question—*who eats, who's eaten*—always unanswered till we gather at the last table for the final meal together, all of us decked out in our odd costumes, our feathers, fur, skin, scales, colors.

I love you, Teddy, my sweet Teddy-pie, coo-coos Timothy Treadwell, the Grizzly Man, to his neighbor at the table, a two ton, shaggy brown beast with fingernails longer than Freddy Kruger's. *Lubs you, too*, Br'er Bear growls back. Then the two of us, my love, strolling home from the Grizzly Man flic, on Norfolk Street, between Stanton and Rivington, opposite a lot strewn with the remains of an apartment building in the last stages of being consumed, the lower east side of New York City, not too far from where Norfolk crosses Delancey and the real estate abruptly strives to be gentrified and trendy, but here mounds of garbage in black plastic sacks piled at the curb, a busy traffic of rats back and forth from lot to bags, bag to bag, even though it's not quite dark yet. Here on Norfolk, I get my flash. *Eureka*. These urban rats big as grizzly bears in the movie, Alaskan grizzlies small as these rats, depending on your point of view, your distance, your hunger, your place at the table. A roach, a star.

Night Manager

He keeps her waiting over an hour in the icy hotel room. She can't figure out the radiator. She's freezing. Stays in her coat until she decides she might be warmer in bed. In spite of the cold, she asks herself should I undress or keep my clothes on. How cozy should I make this. Will he stay interested if things too easy. Too hard. Nearly asleep when she hears a knock, covers herself to let him in. A guest emergency, he apologizes, smiling from the foot of the bed as he undresses. She's not curious about the details, she's cold again, sitting up, quilt pulled to her chin. Shouldn't this business feel more glamorous. New Year's Eve rendezvous with a tall, dark, handsome man. New man. New place where he's the night manager, but he can't get the heat going, either. Damned thermostats, he complains. As if to compensate for keeping her waiting and his lack of success with the heating system, he's very busy, eager, positioning her body this way and that. Surprising tingles, friction there and there, but just as frequently the rolling over, squatting, kneeling, throws off the bedclothes, exposes warm parts of her unhappily to bitter air. In a year this hotel will be gutted, totally renovated inside and out. Walking past she almost won't recognize it. Did she answer the door in her underwear or wrapped in a towel or naked under her coat. Remembers shivering out loud, *Brrr,* in the dark as she felt her way back from the bathroom, grateful for the warmth of his lean bulk when she slipped under the covers. Three months into the New Year, her period gone missing for two and a half of them when she tells him she's pregnant. He had smiled, asked no questions, promised to marry her. The wife and three kids not mentioned when he offers. This is the exact moment she's sure. Though she'd never really been not sure. Not him. Not his smile. Never. Wife and kids or not. No way, Jose. Instantly regretted telling him she's pregnant. He's not the one she needed to tell. Her ex, with his live-in girlfriend the one she wanted to tell. Proof after years of trying, trying and failing with him, her body's still alive. When she loses the baby, there's no one she wants to tell. Certainly not a new man she's begun seeing. How long would he remain curious if she says: some days I stand in the tub shivering. Hot water's run out, no more blood to wash down the drain, shivering, teeth chattering, but I can't move out from under the shower, can't turn it off.

Close

The twins born so alike that their doting mother, blessed be her memory, tied a ribbon around one infant's chubby ankle to tell them apart. Red, the ribbon's color, also served as a name, and aside from the red ribbon always visible on one twin's body, they grew up identical into nearly identical lives, until at the age of twelve, Red contracted a terrible disease. A barrage of radiation, medicine and prayers spared her life but not without leaving behind a sterile womb. Seven years later her twin Rachel gave birth to twins and presented one of the boys to her beloved sister to raise as her own son, a gift so generous and unprecedented it was recorded in the *Book of Perfect Intentions* and Red received honorable mention in the same volume for the generous lack of bitterness she displayed with no choice but to be on the receiving end of the gift. Because the thought of separating their separated boys unbearable as the thought of losing the nearly mystical companionship the twin sisters enjoyed, they all resided for many years under the same roof, one unit of three, one of two, a single happy family. The arrangement worked far better than town gossips predicted and might have lasted longer, except one afternoon while her sister was out shopping, Red (many say the ribbon's color doomed her) decided that sharing the penis of her twin's husband would place very little strain on the generosity of a sister able to share one of her babies. But as everybody knows, husbands are not babies, and the family's domestic arrangements rapidly deteriorated. A secret at first, the sexual trespassing never exactly confessed but allowed to leak out in dribbles. One morning Rachel awakens with wet cheeks, another morning wet feet, then she and the others paddle daily in a slough of jealousy, re-criminations, despair. No one likes anyone anymore, and during a particularly vicious exchange of the dozens one boy hollers, *Yo Mama's a ho* and his twin curses back, *She your Mama, too,* and from that moment on the sons and their sons and their son's sons, even unto the present generation, have waged murderous wars upon one another, perpetuating the slaughter and chaos that give humanity such a bad name.

Party

I go up to Aunt May's wheelchair. She gives me her crinkly hand and I take it. Why are you sprouting warts and whiskers I want to ask her, looking down to find Aunt May's tiny green eyes twinkling in the folds of her moon face, the same pitted, pale flesh of the hand my pale hand squeezes, not too hard, not testing for bones I'm very curious about. Are they brittle or soupy soft or sea-changed altogether to foam like is stuffed inside cloth animals to hold their shape. Draped by bead necklaces dangling to her waist, her hips snug in a sequined flapper dress hemmed with fringe that starts at her knees and almost touches the silver buckles of her shoes, May smiles at me from a sepia-toned photo. No. That's not true. Same smile but May smiles it here, now, her hand in mine, during this celebration of her 83rd birthday, although unbeknownst to everybody at the party (and everyone at the party in the old photo) the surgeon forgot a metal clip in May's gut last week that's festering and will kill her next Christmas Eve. Not one party and then another and another. It's all one big party. Life ain't nothing but a party, May grins at me after I sugar her cheek, dance her hand, the long strings of fringe swish, swishing, brushing my trouserleg as she swirls out, spins, spools in, jitterbugging, camel walking, fox trotting, buzzard lope. My, my, Miss May. Oh-blah-dee. Watch out, girl. You have only eighty-three years or eight months or eight seconds to live before the party's over and the flashbulb freezes you forever, portions of the brownish photo the color of batter I used to lick from my finger after swiping it around the mixing bowl when my Grandmother, your cousin, your fine running partner, light, bright and almost white as you, May, finished pouring her cake in a pan, set the pan in the oven to bake and turned me loose on that bowl. Don't miss none, she'd grin. Get it all, Mr. Doot.

Automatic

They stole my money, my father says. I know exactly what you mean, man, I could have responded, but don't want to get him started on the frozen poem of frustration and rage he can't help reciting, stanza by stanza, because the thieves won't send him the prizes their letters declare he's won. I've come to take away his car keys. Or rather do what our worried family has decided, Ask for his car keys. We'd tried before. No way, Jose, he let us know. Me and that old girl automatic. Drive this whole city blind-folded. Today it's as if he knew before I knocked, someone would be coming by and there would be less of him left as soon as he opened his door, so he's reminding me, whatever my good intentions, that I'm also just like those others who'd lied, stripped and stolen things from him his entire life and aren't finished yet, vultures circling closer and closer, withholding his prizes, picking his bones clean because an old black man too tired to shoo them off anymore. His quick mind leaving him fast but thank goodness my father no pack rat. Until the end his apartment fairly neat. He keeps only the largest letters in their boldly colored, big print envelopes guaranteeing a Corvette or condo in Acapulco or million in cash mega prize. Beside his bed and on the kitchen table large stacks of these lying motherfuckers that taunt and obsess him, his last chance, a glorious grand finale promised though how and when not precisely spelled out in the fine print. He never quite figures out the voices on the other end of his daily 800 calls are robots. Curses the menus white women's voices chirp. His response to my request he surrender his keys gentler. A slightly puzzled glance, a smile breaking my heart, No, Daddy, *no*. *Don't do it*, I'm crying out helplessly, silently, as he passes me the keys.

Dear John

If this were a movie, her scent would perfume the letter. No-body sitting out there in movie darkness would be able to smell it but everybody would guess her perfume's there and understand that the one up here on the big screen, me, slowly raising the letter towards my unhappy mug means I'm pained by loss and yearning and can't resist the urge to inhale one last time whatever intimate trace of lost love the letter confides. The audience would recognize instantly the image of a man facing the music of unre-quited love, an experience perhaps some of them have suffered, but everybody on this night out or matinee performance, willing to pay the price of a ticket to suffer it vicariously, and maybe all of the above is why I blow my nose in the Dear John letter, even though the paper's uncomfortably stiff, noisy, not very absorbent, and preserves intact a gooey mess a bit like yoke seeping from a cracked egg, I think when I peek before crumpling the once upon a time crisp white sheet of computer bond. Obviously silly paper for anyone to blow a nose on/in, but she was a silly woman and I'm a silly man to have relinquished even a smidgen of my heart to silly her, but silly is as silly does, so live and learn, brotherman, I console myself and smirk at the audience as I re-open the letter then refold it neatly to sandwich the snot more securely, wonder-ing if I'm holding an original in my hand or if she mailed the copy—her new laser printer so good you can't tell the difference —because she duplicates all her correspondence, retaining a set for her writer's file to be sold and archived when she's famous— silly is as silly does—and I honk into it again.

Writing

All the years I never learned to write. Stop. Start. A man on a bicycle passes down Essex Street in the rain. Gray. Green. Don't go back. You won't write it any better. More. You can only write more or less. That's all. A man in a greenish gray slicker pedals down Essex in a slashing downpour. Leaves behind a pale brushstroke of color that pulsates, coming and going as you stare into empty slants of rain. A flash of color left behind. Where is the man. Where gone. What on his mind. The color not there really. Splashed and gone that quick. A bit of wishful thinking. A melancholy painting on air. Do not go back. It doesn't get better. Only more. Less. The years not written do not wait to be written. Wait nowhere. No. An unwritten story is one that never happens. A story is never until after the writing. Before is pipe dream. Something lost you wish you hadn't or wish you had. Gone before it got here. There is no world full of unwritten stories waiting to be written. Not even one. To hang people's hopes on, the hope that their story will be revealed one day, worth something, true, even if no one else can see it or touch it, a beautiful story like in that girl's sad eyes on the subway, her life story real as anyone's, as real as yours, her eyes say to me, a story no one has written, desperate to be written. Never will be. Rain blurs the image of a man steadfastly splashing down Essex Street on his bike through driving rain, rain whose force and weight any second will disintegrate the gray sheet of paper on which the figure's drawn, a man huddled under a gray green slicker who doesn't know he's about to disappear and take his world with him. Except for a stroke of gray green hovering in my eyes like it did the day we crossed the dunes and suddenly, for a moment, between steep hills of sand I saw framed in the distance what I thought might be a sliver of the sea we'd come so far to find.

Hit and Run

He doesn't totally think the asshole pedestrian crossing a busy street against the light deserves to die. More like this very large, very shiny, very expensive vehicle gives its driver some rights, too, the goddamned ass-kicker note humping him every month, no choice really in a city full of terrorist potholes worse than Iraq and born fucking poor die fucking poor anyway so why not go for it, better than wiped out in an ambush, smoking dead beside your blown to bits Honda or mashed Hyundai, they all sound alike, look alike, dead cause you're too cheap to put out for armor, for speed, for 8-way adjustable leather bucket seats recycling your comfort zone at a push of a button, sound tracks of your action movie life jamming through so many speakers you forget how many or where the fuck they are, your tunes you pick apart and remix to let everybody know its you coming, you locked and loaded a bad motherfucker rocking the block, a serious investment in this pussy copping wagon no doubt about it though it's not quite yours yet, just forget about it, hooked up in this baby's cockpit, this steel joint wild bull elephant balls charging down Grand Street, the punk's eyes don't believe it, you can't just run people over in a civilized country, eyes screaming, *No. No. Stop*, still hoping nobody really crazy enough to do it, you know, get in big trouble, court trouble, bail bonds, lawyers, judge, the slam, maybe unhappy ever after all the days of your natural born life, oh yeah, yeah I hear you talking my man and maybe I'm fucking up bad but you, you sleaze bag straggling in the middle of a busy public street wacko where you got no right to be, you bitch, you're toast.

Gait

From the window seat of Clandestino he watches people pass by on Canal Street. He's become a reader of gait. That's g-a-i-t, not the other g-a-t-e, he's explained more than once, though in fact, these two words *gait* and *gate* with different meanings and different spellings have in common more than an identical sound. They share among other things the etymological root *path*, he'll go on to point out if he finds someone who seems content to listen to an old man ramble. *Ramble.* You see. Ramble's a kind of gait. Fits me to a "T," I must confess. Gait reveals character, gait discloses truth. There are idle gaits, broken gaits, upright, sneaky or crooked gaits. Look at her marching by, tiny goose-step after tiny goose-step marching. Such a little thing, too, in her tall heels, short skirt, low blouse between those two suited fellows who tippy-tip as if on eggshells. Lots of Asians on Canal. An ancient female one passes doubled over at the waist, each body part advancing separately, cards slowly dealt from a deck of pain. Many european nationalities he swears he can identify by gait. Gait a gate, afterall. Gait opens an unknown space ahead, closes traveled space behind. The second glass of Languedoc as usual speeding his thoughts. Years stream by. Their gaits familiar, predictable. A giddy sense of lift, then fear of falling. Soon the sky will be black over the high, dark fence of buildings across Canal. Light fading as it fades every evening, but he never studies the speed of light's gait, light's footfalls more silent than the silent others through Clandestino's window.

Breath

Sometimes you feel so close it's like we're cheek to cheek sucking the breath of life from the same hole.

In a few hours the early flight to Pittsburgh because my mom's life hanging by a thread. Thunder and lightning you're sleeping through, cracks the bedroom's dark ceiling like an egg. About 4:00 a.m. I need to get up. Drawing a deep breath, careful as always to avoid stress on the vulnerable base of my spine when I shift my weight in bed, I slide my butt toward the far edge, raise the covers and pivot on one hipbone to a sitting position, letting my legs fold over the bed's side to find the floor, still holding my breath as I get both feet steady under me and slowly stand, hoping I didn't bounce the mattress, waiting to hear the steady pulse of your sleep before I exhale.

In the kitchen a yellowish cloud presses against the window. A cloud oddly lit and colored it seems by a source within itself. A kind of fog or dust or smoke that's opaque, unsettling, until I understand the color must come from security lights glaring below in the courtyard. It's snow. Big flakes not falling in orderly rows, a dervishing mob that swirls, lifts, goes limp, noiselessly spatters the glass. Snow obscuring the usual view greeting me when I'm up at crazy hours to relieve an old man's panicked kidneys or just up, up and wondering why, staring at blank, black windows of a hulking building that mirrors the twenty storey bulk of ours, up prowling instead of asleep in the peace I hope you're still enjoying, peace I wish upon the entire world, peace I should know better by now than to look for through a window, the peace I listen for beside you in the whispering of our tangled breaths.

Writing (2)

Sometimes I'm sad I'm not the best writer in the world. I'm even sadder that my son is serving a life sentence in prison. I know these things have nothing to do with each other. If I became the best writer in the world, it wouldn't get my son out of prison. Though I'd be ecstatic if my son were free, it wouldn't cure the other sadness. Less. More. What do less or more mean when it comes to sadness. Someone said a full portion's a full portion, no matter the size of the portion. But that's not really helpful or true either, and even if true, wouldn't help. Finish your banana. Gaze out your ninth floor window at the skyline of the big city which a gray cloud is either descending upon or rising from. The cure for bad writing is to stop doing it. Set yourself free. The cure for prison—ha, ha—is also when the sentence ends. Neither of which is true, nor funny, not an improvement upon sadness, except never never never is it required of you to mean exactly what you write because you can always erase it and try to begin again or not begin again even though it doesn't change sadness either way, the sadness that's most real when in fact it's not yours and can only be imagined, the way once upon a time in your dreams you imagined your children's lives might be perfect or at least a whole god damn lot better off than you'll ever be or do until one day you find yourself writing about an altogether different state of affairs than you ever would or could have imagined. And not very well. Not even close.

Thirteen

Now comes the thirteen story. Thirteen the day of my son's birth. Lucky. Unlucky. How could it happen. On the 13th, one fifteen year old kills another. The chance of that one particular thing happening small as a single breath in the universe. The universe the size of the chance against the possibility of that moment undoing itself, never happening, going away. With two Arizona lawyers, my son, his mother I'd stopped loving and me in it, the car speeds south to north, Phoenix to Flagstaff. I'm driving, listening to one lawyer speak when the other, suffering unbeknownst to us from his own lonely addiction, interjects something about too bad it's not *Massachusetts* which he pronounces *Massa-two-sits* before he resumes staring out the window. Arizona wants to start executing juveniles, the other lawyer continues. The state's looking for the right kid to kill. A black kid would suit them perfectly. Plea bargaining our only chance to save your son's life.

Years before I'm able to sit through this ride again, before I can speak to anyone about Arizona's jails full of Mexicans and Indians, the zigzag mountain peaks stitching sky to earth, sumptuous oil spills of sunset, one sudden burst of rain battering dry plains like sheets of tears. On the last night of a Western tour, returning from the Grand Canyon, a group of fifteen-year-olds stay at an Arizona motel. Next morning my son's roommate found stabbed to death. My son missing. For days presumed dead, tortured, buried by some madman in the Arizona desert or mountains. Then my son calls home. We fly to Arizona to turn him in. Plead. Life the best we can hope for. After long silence Freddy Jackson's "You are my lady," my son's favorite song, playing on the car radio as we head to Flagstaff. One note breaks me down. Like one shooting star mote of plaque can explode a brain. One instant of insanity explode two boys' lives. Sheets of tears. You only get one chance. That's all a father gets with a son. A child's life in your hands once. That's it. Once. He was born in New Jersey and I took classes to assist at his birth, but some clown passed out the day before, so on the 13th the delivery room off limits for fathers and I missed the moment the earth cracked and she squeezed out his bloody head.

Message

A message in red letters on the back of a jogger's T shirt passed by too quickly for me to memorize exactly. Something about George Bush going too far in his search for terrorists and WMD's. A punch line sniggering that Bush could have stayed home and found the terrorist he was looking for in the mirror. I liked it. The message clever I thought and jacked the idea for my new line of black lettered T-shirts: America went way too far looking for slaves. Plenty niggers in the mirror for sale.

One Person Threw a Rock...

At an emergency press conference yesterday in City Hall, Chief William Parker of the LAPD offered his analysis of the exploding Watts riot: *One person threw a rock and then, like monkeys in a zoo, others started throwing rocks.* How many rocks, a reporter asks. How many monkeys, another asks. The next one asks, Could the ruckus maybe be a movie set, maybe. Then one asks, Have you ever visited a zoo or a jungle, Chief. Before Chief Parker can answer, a reporter follows up with, Have you ever visited Watts, Chief Parker, and the Chief cuts his eyes at that reporter, whispers to an aide, Get his badge number. And speaking of badge numbers, Chief Parker, an alert stringer from a wire service back East asks, What's the rationale for officers removing their badges when they wade into crowds with their nightsticks. Chief Parker smiles, That's old school policy. Now my boys wear big American flag decals on their helmets and flags sewn on their sleeves to identify themselves. Chief Parker, would you comment please, Sir, on the sentiments of your colleague, Paris Prefect of Police Grimaud, a poet by the way, who will characterize the students riots of May '68 as "the last great literary revolution in Europe." I don't speak French, the Chief replies, Next question. Back to the rocks you mentioned earlier, Chief Parker, the pain-in-the ass reporter says, Were rocks found near the bodies of any of the 32 dead Negro victims or 3 dead white victims...

Unfortunately, the black box recording of the news conference ends here with a thunderous crash. The lone survivor of City Hall's collapse, a janitor, saved it seems because he exited the building to dispose of a plastic sack full of trash he'd gathered from the press briefing room just moments before disaster struck, had this to add when interviewed: All I know, Cap'n, I heard one dem white folks ax a question, den anudder one ax anudder question den deys all axing questions and next thing happen I'm dumping trash and dem old walls start to crackle and come tumbling down.

One on One

Neck craned at an awkward angle, arms stretched unnaturally, burning above his head, he's so intent on threading white nylon cord through slots in the iron hoop's underside, he wobbles and almost falls from atop the garbage can he'd pulled beneath the perforated metal backboard. Third net in three weeks replaced. With his back to the court now he sits on a bench and stares at traffic on the East River. Sea Princess, Zephyr, yellow water taxis, a cop speedboat, long garbage barge. He's goddamn sick and tired of being chumped and dissed in his lonely crusade to improve one small detail of this raggedy-ass neighborhood. The payback he's planning drastic, maybe even a bit crazy he thinks, but things way past fucked up here. His plan makes sense if only for his own peace of mind: punish one of the wannabe Shaqs who pull on the net. The fact the guy he punishes will be more or less his color and stuck here like him gives him a small headache. But no point making his point in some other part of the city where lines on the courts always painted and rims always netted. Not his fault he loves the game, loves the rules of the court. Hurting someone who broke the rules wouldn't be personal, it would be about love, he'd explain to the black or brown perpetrator and maybe not shoot him, maybe just poke the gun in his face and scare him, scare the others, let the guilty one slide this once, but he never gets the opportunity to decide life or death because the high flyer who'd just dropped from hanging on the net sees him coming, sees something in the other's eyes and with a B-ball quick hand snatches the gun waved in his face. Pow. Blew that old nigger away, boy.

Manhole

On South Street where it parallels the East River, only a hundred yards or so from the water, next to a tall cyclone fence enclosing a parking lot for emergency vehicles, a stubby guy, rubbing his hairy-backed hands together briskly, clambers out of a manhole to join his partner who leans on a huge white slurping tank truck. Both workers in official coveralls so my taxes pay their salaries and I think that means we're on the same page and think in these uptight times a little humor always helps and think it might be funny when I cruise past to smile and point at the open manhole and say, Ah-hah. So that's where you white guys come from, and I do say it but they don't appreciate my joke and I surely don't think it's funny either when I glance back and catch the one beside the truck dragging a pistol out the back pocket of his baggy yellow jumpsuit. Eyes wide, asshole squeezed tight, I accelerate the pace of my jogging. Hear over my shoulder, Run, nigger, run—you better run, you black shine, and then the unmistakable pop which takes me down sprawling on the asphalt, hitting hard as if I'd been pitched from a speeding drive-by, but I'm not dead I'm rolling, rolling fast to my feet, haul-assing like a turkey through the corn for cover round a bend as if a bullet couldn't catch me if it wanted to. No laugh meter in the vicinity so I don't know whose joke funnier, mine or theirs. One man, one vote, but one of me, two of them and bullets trump ballots anyway just like Malcolm said, but maybe I get the last laugh because the white guy on a bench staring out at the East River, traffic reports buzzing from his tiny radio, still sits there on my return leg and I crackle his eyeglasses into the bridge of his nose with a precise, surprise elbow, all this in not much more than the usual 45 minutes my jog consumes, a sure sign the weather's warming, the city cleaning up for another long, hot summer of being the biggest, baddest apple in the world.

Wall

Beside one exterior wall of the house in Brittany, a beigish, stucco, two storey, windowless wall the morning sunlight strikes first when there is sunlight, a gravel walk leads to a small back garden enclosed by tall hedges. Along one edge of the walk, to divide gravel from grass, an eight-inch high border stretches like an unbroken row of miniature headstones, one rounded top after another, alike as if shaped by a cookie cutter. Bedded next to this low, gray wall, a line of rose bushes, each planting separate and scrawny. Some seem merely a handful of sparsely leaved twigs jammed in the ground, others not much bigger bear copious roses larger than my fist. All of them nod and quiver in the early light, a fitful breeze cued as always by the sea's proximity.

I tell you this in painstaking detail because after I fix coffee and carry it with my tablet and pens outside and settle on a reclining chair positioned on the gravel walk so it's sheltered from wind by the bare, beige wall and also exposed to catch the sun's first warmth, if there is any warmth, a voice will say to me: *No.* No matter how many words you write or how carefully you choose them, no one's able to see the world through another person's eyes. Another's eyes negate yours, verify the fact a world you will never get to see is moving along quite well, thank you, whether you're present or absent. The world commences just beyond the margin of your vision, with what you don't see, and the rest is simply you, what you do see, your separate gaze of no consequence, impermanent, arbitrary as what you don't see, no matter how closely you look or another looks at you.

Equals

Tall, skinny, freckled Mr. Brooks no more the real Mr. Brooks as I write him now than I was real to him in his 5th grade math class, a brown kid, a rarity in Pittsburgh's Liberty elementary school. Mr. Brooks, who went out of his way to teach and befriend me until I refused to believe zero times a number equals zero. How could you have less than you started with. A shiny dime stuffed down in my pocket and somebody comes along and multiples it by zero and my pocket's empty. Huh-uh. No way. My reasoning impeccable, unshakable. Zero times my dime all you want and I'd still own my dime.

After Mr. Brooks whacked me with a ruler for being stupid or obstinate or arrogant or a smart aleck or whatever combination and permutation of the above he figured I was displaying to the class by repeating my knuckle-head idea, it took me forty years to make my peace with numbers. Alone one early morning in my kitchen, counting slices of banana dropping into a bowl of granola, I realized I was reciting a kind of poem…1-2-3… to quiet the vast, unfathomable silence engulfing me. Took longer than forty years, I guess, to make peace with Mr. Brooks because when he sprang unexpectedly from the audience I'd just read my fiction to in California, I didn't quite hug him like lost father, lost son but immediately reminded him he'd hit me long ago and called me Jack, his name for me though my name's John. Didn't go as far as saying you killed the passion I might have discovered for numbers. I shut up because given the look in his eyes, I'd stung Mr. Brooks enough, though not as much as his ruler stung the back of my hand.

Plot

He found the ring walking at dawn (*him* walking, not the ring) low tide on a rocky, kelp-blackened beach about two miles from his friends' rented cabin deep in the woods. *This crusty old thing worth half a million, I bet*, his astounded, delighted, too-good-to-be-true, professional antique dealer's estimate, never guessing that sum would induce his friends to plot to murder him and steal the ring.

He might be dead now except that after a year of casual intimacy, just as he had no inkling of his friends' desperate, ruthless longing for wealth, they had no suspicion of his sexual preferences. Things might have turned out quite differently if it had been the husband not the wife who slipped into his bed the second night of his visit begging for love. But it was her. Making it easier for him, despite her sobbed tale of a husband's impotence and cruelty, to deny her plea for even a small bout of physical intimacy, thus frustrating the couple's plan to seduce him into an incriminating exchange of DNA that would have served as proof positive of a perfidious guest's trespass, evidence mitigating an enraged husband's fatal retaliation. When the husband, called away overnight by a sudden (fake) emergency, burst into the guest's bedroom waving a dragoon-sized pistol and reeking of vodka, he found his wife and guest less than fully clothed, but except for one brief, awkward scuffle, neither had laid a hand on the other. Rushing at her husband the woman shouted, *No... no...wait*, and in the ensuing melee, no surprise that someone shot dead. The visitor doesn't get to fuck either wife or husband, and alas, his hosts no longer possess each other as sexual partners (who knows how much truth in the wife's tale of abuse). The story could end here, happily ever after, with the guest living large on proceeds from the priceless ring, but that leaves out a twist. His visit's abrupt termination prevented the guest from revealing two secrets he had intended to release from the closet during his stay, the second secret being that the ring's value a fiction concocted to entertain friends.

Bereaved

After the funeral, after canapés and hard liquor at my brother's house, I find a face, one like mine starting to line, a quietly attractive woman's face, a guest not family, not familiar, a woman whose eyes meet mine and like mine consider and dismiss in about the time it takes to blink twice, a love, a life we could have shared, and in a second, slightly longer last look at each other, we exchange sadnesses, regrets, not so much mourning the ones gone or the others who will go soon, go next, what my eyes asking and maybe hers, too: would anyone choose to come here if they knew beforehand what happens here, if they had a choice.

Oh Shit

Art worth a shit these days comes from bums not worth a shit but their shit sells for incredible money and then the shit-faced bums got the nerve to treat everybody like shit. A shitty business I got myself shitted up in. Big shits who own the galleries talking shit like they know Soho from Picasso. Little shits run wild till shit hits the fan. Cops and reporters everywhere like they care when a shit ODs on coke, on shitty little girls or shitty little boys. Like anybody gives a shit if a shithead's dead or in jail or out on bail, just so the shits squeeze out more shitty stuff keeps shit rolling in. My boy Darnell got shit for brains. *Sorry, man, he says, my shit not turning me on no more, man,* whining at me for months in his Alvin chipmunk voice from burned out nostrils. Wants to show his shit in some shitbag Paris dump, because he knows my passport fucked and I won't be all over his shit over there. Shitty nigger wants a vacation is what it is. Now. Now when his shit's gold. Gold, you shit. Shit, Darnell. Get your black ass up off the shitty floor, man. Move, man. Close your eyes, man. Close your mouth. Move something, D. What's up with this shit, bro. Why you doing this shitty thing to me, Darnell.

Pills

To be large then small. To be a person setting out on a journey that seems boundless, endless, then to be someone who sees nothing ahead, only narrowing space going nowhere except to the end. She closes her eyes. Sees a painting of the sea across which blue and white waves actually move. Twenty-three pills a day. A confusion of shapes, colors, sizes, names her daughter arranges when she comes to help, lining up paper cups and saucers of pills so she'll take the right ones daily and keep herself alive. Three times a week or so her daughter visits, she thinks, and thinks the thinking thoughts business getting like days and weeks, hard to tell them apart, hard to be sure when one stops and another starts, she thinks, but anyway, once a week or so she drops a day's worth of pills into the toilet. Her prescription, her cure. She's the doctor. Smiles stupidly when she finishes the job just like doctor what's his name smiles at the end of office visits. Happier dumping pills than swallowing pills one by one to the last burp and gag and bitter aftertaste, happier flushed away hand in hand in the colorful swirl down the drain than when she takes pill after pill and they make her sick, or as well as she's ever going to be, the doctor says, but I'll get better soon, she smiles to herself, watching the last pill disappear.

Martyr

God's wonders never ceasing. A child, a mere girl of five or six begs not for the torture to end, but to be scalded again with the others, her tender flesh peeling, defenseless before the onslaught of boiling water the priests pour over her naked limbs. Yet her soul's untouched, cries out not in agony but joy, asking only to be returned to the bosom of her Christian family, united with them as they cross to the Kingdom that no earthly power can deny. Moved in spite of themselves, satan's saffron-robed minions restore the tiny, quivering body to her mother's arms. The poor child's flesh, once pale and pure as driven snow, blistered now, the soles of her feet blackened and torn by the terrible mountain, the many, many crude steps carved in rock we ascended to reach this pinnacle of suffering. So high, so far from city crowds the officials would turn against us by shaming us, defaming our faith with the spectacle of apostasy. Hidden here because these Shoguns, though they scorn us, fear God's strength inside our frail flesh. Fear His truth will shine forth no matter how ingeniously they torment us. God teaching the multitudes that with faith even the weak and helpless can endure every horror evil men invent. A child's pure soul undefeated by the fires of Hell, though I, King's envoy and Chief of the Jesuit band, quake and cringe, hung by my heels above a pit of steaming dung, and renounce my Father's name.

Ruins

Pepe, dead ten years now, in his late sixties when he wrote a phrase I admire, a phrase translated from his Spanish as *ruins of her backside*. Perhaps because I'm over sixty now myself, a long ago student of Pepe and like him a fiction writer, I'm remembering that striking phrase and recite it to my wife.

Stunning, isn't it, I say. How perfectly Pepe's image evokes the sadness of the body.

Did you ever consider how his wife might have felt reading those words in her husband's book. Words that expose and judge and take away her privacy forever. The cruelty of writers is unbelievable. How could he say such an awful thing.

Whoa. Hold on. I didn't write the words. And in the novel they're thought, not spoken. And Pepe's not the one thinking the words. It's a sixty-ish man, a character whose name I've forgotten, in bed watching his wife undressing or maybe she's dressing for work in the morning. Either way the point is the man's touched by his wife's nakedness. You know. Flesh as site of eros and death. I hear tenderness in the words. The guy's identifying with his wife. The ruins are everybody's flesh. The flesh that betrays us all. I admire Pepe's unflinching gaze.

But why is the wife's backside displayed for readers to gawk at. Why not Pepe's. C'mon. Be honest. You're just defending Pepe's right to write whatever he damn well pleases. Even if it's waving his poor wife's aging, bare ass around in public.

My wife never met Pepe nor Miranda, his wife and love of

48

his life who had survived Pepe's passing less than a year. Nor read Pepe's novels as far as I know and sometimes I wonder if she really reads mine, since her upset with Pepe is a replay of numerous upsets with me when she confuses my fiction with our lives. What do you think, Dear Reader. Does she have a case.

Creole

At first, though she knew no one would be walking the wooded path above the sea, not in this weather, not at this hour, she listens for help, lies still as death beneath his great, dark weight, a cold splash of mud under her shoulders the only sound when he hurls her down and pins both her wrists above her head in one iron hand, the other hand yanking, ripping, stroking her naked below her waist. She never considers screaming. Chose this path, didn't she—didn't he—because nothing happens here, nothing ever disturbs the quiet of this secluded place until his hoarse whispers cut through white noise of breakers and wind to erase the silence. His pidgin French almost incomprehensible. French thick, wet, slippery as the tongue he slides in and out of her ear. Saying she's beautiful or she's a beast or saying he's one. Promising not to hurt. Saying love, whore, saying he's a good father, saying names, saying sorry, please, no hurt, sorry, saying he must have her, must, must. Like weather, like a storm atop her. Elemental. Sudden. Quick. Tidal rushes of heavy breathing, grunts and moans, chop, chopped phrases panted, hissed. Raw, wild stink engulfing her. A terrible life, she thinks. Homeless. A wanderer. Exile. Thief. Wants to instruct him two wrongs don't make a right. Wants to plead innocent. Pardon his droll French she might smile at in a movie. Or cry. Or pity. He lifts her hips, balls them tight in huge fists, lets them drop back into sucking black mud, mashing, rolling her to match rhythms of his lonely frolic. If some of his mangled words true, maybe he's not the worst kind, the dangerous ones who don't know better or do and don't care. This coupling on a deserted hillside above the ocean may end not entirely unlike a dance she saw one night in a club, two people—one black, one white—performing it and why can't she recall its catchy name.

Cleaning Up

I was jogging on the green shoulder of a country road, enjoying the quiet and solitude of a bygone time, a world lost forever it seems except for rare moments when nature helps us recall the peace and plenty of our original state, then suddenly, directly in my path, a slightly squashed, blue-banded plastic water bottle appeared. I considered my options—around, over, kick it aside. Of course I could have slowed, picked it up and carried it till I could dispose of it properly. Didn't. A few strides later admitted to myself I should have picked it up, would have if I'd believed someone was watching. And thought how sad it would be to become a hopeless case. To skip good deeds because no one applauds. To sink to the level of people incapable of doing the right thing for its own sake. The incorrigible ones who toss beer cans from car windows.

A few days later, just beyond a heap of horse dung steaming like a judgment on this fallen earth, the bottle is still there. And then I encounter more... six... eight... ten at least in a half mile stretch, each identical almost to the first, unpleasant likenesses breeding, multiplying. I don't disturb them, but promise myself to return. Return with friends and remove every last one of them. We'll dress in white like angels, wear surgeons' masks and rubber gloves. Bring rakes to comb them from the grass. Large black garbage bags to haul them away in our trucks.

Cubans

This whole story came to me in a kind of flash. It's short. May I read it to you. Of course. I always enjoy your stories.

Broad daylight, Sunday, and the beach crowded with families, so when I say, Let's go skinnydipping, she thinks I'm kidding. I nag, tease, nag until she rises on her elbow from the green and white striped towel. "Go. Stop pestering me and go. You go. Not me. Nobody swims naked here and anyway I'm quite happy just lying in the sun."

"If you love me, you'll do it."

"That's blackmail," she hollers, mock frown on her face.

"You don't expect whitemale from me do you," I reply, and she cracks up. Not because my silly punning is funny, but because misfits like us, mock lovers—black male girl, white female boy—need laughter at a time when denunciations, raids, assaults, disappearances are becoming commonplace. *Cubans* our little group calls itself, in coded memory of the victims of an older, failed revolution, the victims of every revolution's backlash when it turns on itself to devour the rebels who spawned it or the rebels it spawns. In a second our suits are off. Around us everybody else begins undressing. They're dancing and singing behind us as we race, two *Cubans* bareass, squealing and giggling on a sunny Puerto Rican beach, blue sky above, blue, blue ocean thundering ahead."

Not much to it really, I guess. Probably not a story yet.

Oh, I like it. Even though your story's sort of blackmail, too. I mean I'm supposed to identify with your *Cubans*, right. Their little moment of breaking the rules. Identify. Or else. Or else terror and death sure to follow, right. Get naked and jump in if you want the revolution to happen. Isn't that what your story's insisting.

My answer a scream. At her, myself. Yelling, Who knows what the fuck's coming next. I sure as shit don't. I don't claim to know jack shit, but we must do something. This is not a story we're in. You can't just lie there. Do something, bitch.

Glass Eye

In order to write the essay his friend requested for a catalogue of the friend's first solo exhibit of glass objects fashioned by a notoriously exacting process called *pâte de verre*, an ancient Egyptian art passed down in his friend's case from grandfather to grandson, he asked the friend to lend him one of his recent sculptures. For three weeks the glass cube has been sitting on his desk where the friend placed it just before the friend flew to Venice for a show that included a few of his pieces. He'd moved the cube only once since the news of the friend's death, lifting it and setting it back quickly, as precisely as he could within the dust print on the desktop. He'd been impressed by the 8-inch cube's weight—was it water frozen to ice frozen to glass frozen to absolute zero to produce some super heavy, hyper-dense alloy of transparent iron. This freakish substantiality contrasting with a fragile chaos of grains, bleeding colors, twisting lines of force when he peered inside the cube. Sunken letters, numbers, words float and drift there, exchanging places, a helter-skelter illusion of clashing perspectives inhabiting the silence of a convulsively claustrophobic space.

Years before on Martinique, in a tiny, chilly museum dedicated to Surrealism, he'd been subdued by a collection of everyday items—spoon, cup, coin, eyeglasses, etc.—bizarrely, nearly unrecognizably transformed by the pyroclastic blast of Mount Pele's eruption. The terror of sudden mutation, a howling, screaming transition seemed sealed in the glass display case with the spontaneously created artifacts. The severe geometry of his friend's cube enclosed a similarly stricken world. Time's moment to mo-

ment flow violently sundered, time collapsed, simultaneously frozen and released by a distorting lens, his gaze locked with a glass
eye's unwavering stare, a false window, trap door through which
he plummets endlessly, helpless as something being torn away
from itself, something lost, yearning to be what it isn't, what it
must be. More than imitation, more than a fake something. A
bottomless wish... as if... as if...he's desperate now for words
to jump-start the stalled essay... as if dead flesh could return as
bread and wine. No. As if a glass eye hiding blindness at last
could be seen as real, at last see itself.

Evolution

It would be wonderful if animals could say things about the world...But they just don't.

Geoffrey Pullam, linguist

Before we arrived in the forest to study chimpanzee behavior, compare it to ours, and initiate communication with these members of the group of great apes whose DNA is closest to man's, no chimpanzee, according to local tribal legend, had ever fallen from the green kingdom of treetops high above the forest floor. Our observations supported the veracity of this curious piece of folklore and one lesson we hoped to gain from the chimpanzees was the secret of their fearless skill and immunity to accident. We captured a dozen chimps, taught them a handful of words, including *fall*. In order to clarify the meaning of fall without compromising the chimp's instinctive sense of immortality, we also taught them the word *sleep*, miming sleep to illustrate where a fall takes them after they sink into the shimmering green sea of leaves and branches and do not return. Seven days after we reintroduced our captive chimps into their natural habitat, the first chimp fell. Some of my colleagues asserted that we'd erred by not teaching the word *death* to the chimps. Others argued *death* far too abstract a concept to introduce into the chimp's rudimentary vocabulary. At this juncture in our research a furious debate ensued over the limits of chimp intelligence and whether or not human language could or should be transmitted to apes, but before we could agree on a course of action, an epidemic of fatal plunges had emptied the trees of chimps.

Imagine a chimpanzee kicked back in its leafy nest constructed high in the branches of a towering tree, imagine the chimp
dreaming the story above, then dreaming up words to end the
story differently.

Raymond Story

It's me, Raymond.

Of course she remembers the name. Then perhaps something familiar in the smile and wonders how she's changed in the twenty-some years since she's last seen this thick, balding stranger with his arms held out toward her. She has not changed enough, it seems, as to be unrecognizable. Or some part of her unchanged. Sprawling red hair. Sea green eyes. Something still slightly cute she hopes got his attention. When she'd first met him, she didn't know the language. *Raymon.* He liked to drop by and drive her places. She'd ride with him through Harlem some afternoons as he conducted what she understood only as *Bizness, Babe.* Clubbing some weekend nights. Raymond not demanding. Occasionally they made love a weird once near the end with another watching, maybe participating—lovemaking without ever becoming exactly lovers. Raymond her guide to a new city. One of the few people she knew in a new country. A very nice, very big car. She remembered the car precisely, without retaining a picture of it. Like his mother she'd never seen, a nervous voice over the phone, an answering machine before such things existed, who would never put her through to Raymond. He'd often return her calls immediately, and she'd always wanted to ask him why his mother didn't hand him the phone instead of saying *I'll give Raymond the message* and hanging up, but her English too poor to ask. Mostly blank pages in the Raymond story she unexpectedly hears herself telling herself for the first time in years and years. What Raymond story will she tell the new man browsing close behind her in the crowded gallery. A

very curious, very jealous man she knows because they had talked a lot already, lots of intense talk maybe the best thing between
them so far. A story about him in the language she'd mastered
now has begun to form itself, write itself, and she's making up
more of it as she steps toward this other, this Raymond surprise,
his empty pages she must fill and erase and fill again before she
turns to answer the new man's questions.

You Are My Sunshine

E-mail from my French translator, Jean-Pierre Richard, asking for clarification of inconsistencies between text of novel *Hiding Place* and family tree appended as preface to novel—particularly the character, Shirley, who in text noted several times as middle child, though on tree she's an oldest child.

Shirley's not either, she's both, I want to respond—not only my sister, not only a character—the world of the novel depends on fact and fiction and I'm just a mediator with no answers or changing answers, always more questions than answers, as curious as you are, Jean-Pierre, a translator like you, who at best attempts to mediate irreconcilable differences. My wife Catherine who's bilingual says she hates it when she's stuck between friends who speak only French and friends who speak only English and she's forced into translating for both groups. Exhausting, she says. Frustrating. Like being pulled apart. I can't relax. Nobody's satisfied. And you feel like you're to blame, don't you, I add to commiserate with her and myself in my chosen/appointed role as go-between for people not from different countries, not speaking different languages exactly but people sharing a country who choose often not to understand or like each other, people who use things like prisons to translate an ancient need to remain separate.

As for your other query, those words in italics are a line from "You Are My Sunshine," a favorite of my Culpepper, Virginia grandfather, John French, who used to sing it to me riding on his shoulders when I was very young. I wish I could translate his singing, Jean-Pierre, but it's as hopeless as translating love into words and sending it in a letter to my son in prison. I can't translate my grandfather's singing, only put words on a page, *You make me happy when skies are gray...*, and hum them softly to myself as I write, the same words by the way that Richard Berry (of *"Louie, Louie"* fame) translated in his fashion and got much of the song right because his version playing in my head brings my son here right beside me, with me, wherever else he must be.

Lost and Found

Nothing reminds him of her. She was everything, then he lost her and now there's nothing. A train rattling, squealing near midnight over the East River to Brooklyn, a mad woman twitching in the seat across the aisle from his, then maybe not mad, a wire in her ear, she thinks she's dancing, dances to nothing he can hear, there is nothing to hear, though in the nothingness surrounding him he's taught himself exactly how to locate the one missing. Clattering F train. The third stop. A grid of streets memorized from a map. First right. Right again. Two blocks. Left. Right, etc.... etc. A route prowled three times in daylight, aching for a glimpse. Afraid of a glimpse. Nothing. Tonight, crouched in a black alley, he will stare up at the fourth floor window again, or if he dares, swoop up and peek in. Like a dark moon spying through the lighted square in the brick wall of the new man's building. She'll be reading late. That won't change. He knows it like he knows the taste of her. The taste like nothing else. Nothing special about rooms up there he's never seen, nothing except she's passing through them, unaware of his eyes, preternaturally unaware of herself yet self-conscious, fretting about some detail of hair or nails or make-up, a nothing, certainly nothing a man's eyes would notice, a man would see nothing but how she fills space, transforms space to what truly matters, all that matters and beyond which there is nothing, an inconceivable nothing if emptied of her.

Some nights when she couldn't sleep, couldn't read, he'd hear her in bed beside him flipping pages of glossy fashion magazines, fat catalogues, flipping fast, faster, then slower, slowly, slowly disappearing into silence, into his dreams of nothing, no one, nothing he remembers now except her presence, lost when he awakens.

Story

He's gotten her used to receiving things from him—cash last birthday, small gifts on holidays, surprises of candy or ice cream, ritual kisses of goodbye or hello, a pinch of her plump cheeks—so when he offers his neighbor's daughter his penis, she'll only hesitate a moment before she lets him wrap her baby fingers around it. Not really much of a stretch from there to the rest—he's a kind, generous man, overpays her oldest brother for trimming his hedges, the father for repairing his car, treats for the younger siblings, teasing gallantries for the mousy wife he employs to watch his daughter so his wife can work three days a week—why wouldn't such a pleasant, exploitable neighbor be trusted alone with his daughter's little playmate. Why wouldn't he be offered ample opportunity to take his time with her, and kindly, leisurely, gently initiate her step by step into the mysteries of his pleasure, though to anticipate the process as seamless is stretching the point, dulling the point, he'd admit, given exciting differences in scale that could not be negotiated without tears or other lubricants—soft smiles, caresses, secret presents, calming allegories of birds and animals. The captivating spell of imagining the story of how he'd use her evaporates the day his daughter complains about *too rough* touching.

Something must have happened at the neighbors, he replies. Let's hope it's just nasty talk she's heard over there. But with those rowdy boys and the wild, brazen little sister, God knows what goes on. Stop sending her to them.

Tell me the truth, please.

Stop working and stay home with her. Or find another sitter.

Why would my baby say it's you, her daddy, hurting her. Please. Tell me what's happening.

Bet her chubby little buddy's telling tales. Scaring her. Confusing her. I'm her father, for Chrissake. Nothing's happening. Nothing to confess.

If no truth in it, why would she make up such a horrible story.

Why would I, I ask myself.

Coo-Coo

I'm learning their lingo. The birds I hear first thing mornings, last thing at night, 10:30, 11:00, my dinner about over, light dying late, dinner late as is the custom this far north in Brittany, birds whose distinctive pigeony coo-cooing frames my days you could say, a presence I can count on afternoons as well while I sit and read in my garden they coo loud and often, especially these mid-July days which I guess might be their mating season because of fierce, invisible rackets exploding deep in thick foliage and the bird's goofy arrogance on the roads, strutting or puttering along, tiny heads bobbing with ghetto, bebop nonchalance till the very last instant before they dodge a car's tires, pale breasts teasing inches above an onrushing windshield, then lifting, fast and furiously miles overhead, their far away cries shattering rural calm. *Mourning doves* or *turtle doves* might be their name in English, and what French calls the birds I have no clue, and really don't care because I'm too busy teaching myself the birds' language. Not phrases or sentences yet. A single word at a time. *Loneliness* the first. I hear *loneliness* at dawn and *loneliness* again at dusk, and in between, no other words I understand yet. Only the frantic beating of wings, endless chasing, one coo-cooing at another whether another listens or not, each solitary cry a sounding of this world's silence that vanishes in another world's silence, every cry the same and different, an eloquent, careful repetition and mocking echo of itself, a language of mirrors I'm trying to learn: coo-coo, coo-coo, coo-coo.

Cry In

I believe I know what *cry out* means. What I'm trying to figure out is *cry in*. A meaning for *cry in* doesn't properly exist, but it should, I think. People often say they're *crying inside*. We all know what they mean. But crying inside is not exactly what I'm trying to get at. People say about this or that situation – *it's a crying shame*, a notion closer to what *cry in* could signify, but not quite, since describing something as a *crying shame* suggests there's been time to reflect and consciously process a reaction. *Cries in,* like *cries out,* just happen. To cry out an instinctive act. A gasp, yelp, holler, exclamation, curse, scream, etc., like an explosion of breath after a kick in the belly. When you cry out, the body's speaking for itself, inventing language for what's unsayable in words. A momentary release, even relief, occurs. A *cry in* happens when something unspeakable forces its way inside. A sudden alien message in your chest, guts. A *cry in* speaks no words. Like crying out, it silences language. The story you've been telling yourself about yourself is demolished. No more story. No more inside and outside. No you. Chaos. And chaos doesn't release or relieve. Chaos seizes you by the throat and shakes you in its teeth till it finishes and you drop. Like the poor woman who owned the Divine Lorraine in Memphis and slammed her head on a desk till her brain exploded after she took the call from the hospital announcing Dr. King, her guest, had died from wounds received on the balcony of her motel.

Don't mind me. I'm not expecting you to follow or agree. I'm just sitting here like Otis on the dock of the bay or the Chinaman on a fence trying to make a dollar out of fifteen cents.

Nothing I can do about the news that hit me yesterday, that *cried in* and wiped out whatever's inside me supposed to deal with bad surprises, supposed to spread bad news as kindly, gently as possible to my heart, liver, lungs, the soles of my feet, my bald head, this whole body I've pulled tight like a quilt round me because I'm cold and wet and shivering, alone as can be with just that *cry in* no one asked me if I wanted to hear, nobody asked me if I was ready.

Short Story

Slowly, slow, tiny sips from a bottle of water after a jog on a hot July morning. Drinking slowly a habit learned the hard way on the hoop court when I was one of the best young bloods and between games one Saturday afternoon some of us robbed ice-cold cases of lemonade from an untended delivery truck and everybody lollygigged in the little shade at one end of the playground, chugging endless lemonade, loud and sweaty and full of ourselves, our luck, our power, our thirst, winners of the last run grinning and bragging, the losers trash talking about other times, next times. Lemonade trickling down my chin, sticky on my bare chest. Lemonade till my stomach bloats and cramps and I lose a whole half day of good ball. A camel forever afterwards. No drink till play's over or tiny, tiny sips slowly. Sixty-five years old now and asking myself if that lesson from the court connects with the drastically pared-down stories I've begun attempting. The parallel's seductive. Teaching myself to cut back on the ambition of long forms. Settling for the satisfaction of well-wrought miniatures.

I still shiver inside, thinking about a game starting up. No plan for handling the speed of the best games. Shuttling through my mind now, they don't pass more swiftly than they did back in the day. Faster than the speed of light. Everything, then nothing, then gone, gone. We were nothing. All the players nothing. Ghosts gliding in from the sidelines. No name. No rep. Everything to prove one more time. Nobody till the games rolling, your legs and heart pumping. Will you get abused or do your thing and hear everybody holler.

Games sweet as cold gallons of stolen lemonade pouring down my throat, and before I notice, the whole bottleful of water is gone. Dizzy when I stand. My legs buckling under me, I nearly fall like my wife's father fell, old, white-haired man, sprawled blinking on the grass. Old enough to know better but jumped up from the table too quick after a good, long meal in our garden.

Scheherazade

We were up to 25 and I was getting weary. And weary's dangerous in the dangerous game we play. Besides being a seriously jealous motherfucker, I read lots of books, so naturally I tagged our game *Scheherazade*, you know, like in the *1001 Arabian Nights*. Only my lady is the storyteller and I ain't no sand nigger who gets offed if his rap's jive. Huh-uh. No way. See, the idea of the game is me cleaning the table, wasting all the motherfuckers who fucked my lady before she started fucking exclusively for me. After she names a dude and describes how they got it on, I go to work. Working on her first, then I exterminate the motherfucker got lucky before I came on the scene. Lemme tell you, man. That girl's got her a dynamite imagination. Her stories better than Viagra. But after 25 I was fraying, Bro. Fraying.

We're up to 25, she says. Only 25 more to go, she smiles, and I groan inside. Maybe 26, she smiles again. Might have forgotten one. Wow, I'm thinking. Rather be plain forgot then remembered as a chump she almost forgot.

Anyways, we got through it. Can't tell stories good as her so I'll skip the details. Just say we perpetrated a whole lotta good loving and there's a whole lotta motherfuckers missing in action out there who thought they was God's gift.

Tonight she goes, I remember one more. One more and we're finished. Clean slate just like you ordered. Oh shit, I'm thinking, but my ears perk up and joint jumps hard cause wit her prodigious memory and nasty mind, I bet she ain't forgot nothing, slut just saving the best story for last, and sure enough she starts a hot tale sounds exactly like a couple nights ago when I'd brought along a little friend of mine to celebrate getting to the end, Sweet Natasha, a Russian gal with a accent cute as her cute red-haired pussy. Quite a session, even better when my lady's telling it, but I'll skip the details, only say bitches inexhaustible, boy. Put the best man to shame. It's that threesome story sure enough, blow by blow, everything we did wit Natasha, and she's about to the part where I'm halfway nodded off and looks up at them bitches still steady whaling away, and all the sudden I'm scared. Starts to shake. Ask myself, Where's this story going. Who's gon bust through the door and kill my sorry ass.

Swimming

After sixty years of never venturing into water deeper than I'm tall, learning to swim in the sea isn't easy. My colleague Bernard couldn't understand why I had a problem with believing water would hold me up. For him the body's buoyancy a simple fact, demonstrated once, convincingly, never questioned since his first time floating alone in the ocean. I felt obliged to explain I'm a sinker—my body's weight relative to its surface area means I'm more like lead than feathers. I'd hoped to impress Bernard by citing the law of physics my body violated, but he shook his head, returned to whatever problem my problem had momentarily distracted him from solving. Bernard's a math/science pragmatist. No frills. Fluent in formulas, manuals and maps. Abrupt occasionally to the point of abrasiveness. No patience often, for daydreamers like me, yet his brief, no-nonsense description of his first time afloat in deep water a kind of reassuring mantra this summer of teaching myself to swim. Not his words. I don't remember his words or repeat his words as I nudge myself inch by inch further from shore, closer to a depth where my feet can't touch bottom unless my head's underwater. It's his silence I chant, not words, to calm and shape my breathing, the silence of a boy floating alone in the ocean the first time, a boy receiving a simple revelation—no metaphysics, no god, no promises, no fear of death—just experiencing how the sea outside unconditionally accommodates the sea inside, on my back, stretched out on a carpet of water, arms extended like oars, feet slowly churning, not bothered by the fact there's nothing solid beneath me, nothing certain except believing nothing's enough.

Long Story

A thousand-page novel by a world famous author has just been announced and will be published this fall. Why so many pages. How many stories crammed in all those pages. One story at a time enough. Human beings can't bear too many stories. One story, even a very short one, can be overwhelming. Particularly when it's the only one someone ever reads. Like the one overwhelming us now. The only one most of us get a chance to read. One story or essentially the same story in a million million slightly varied duplications and recyclings of itself read again and again. Therein lies the secret of story power. Once a story gets repeated enough times it hogs the air other stories need to breathe. Other stories turn blue, wither, disappear. No other story makes much sense unless it tells itself in terms of *the* story. Some smart people have taken to calling certain stories *master narratives*. But *the* story is not the master. It invites other people to master it. The way people are said to master a language— meaning to employ a language to speak their minds and feelings, to communicate with neighbors or ignore neighbors who don't speak it, using it finally to claim a place in the master plan the language speaks. Story power is people power from all the people who keep reading, telling and listening to it till they die. These people are a story's owners and caretakers. Even as it captivates and overwhelms them. They are more important than a story's author. In fact for many stories no author is known because stories don't require authors. Just as they don't require close to a thousand pages. The best ones grow on trees—like apples—like the small one in Eden. See what I mean.

Renovation

It used to be a kind of music, her tinkling a floor above him while he pees downstairs. The two of them delivering in synch, same urge, same simple satisfaction. More than just a happy coincidence for him the rare times when it occurred and he would have hollered up to let her know just that, if he hadn't been sure she'd be embarrassed. The smaller bathroom only a toilet and sink really, off the hallway he'd recently painted, sits directly underneath the elegantly remodeled one upstairs, *extravagantly remodeled*, given their fixed income, he'd come close to reminding her more than once as she chose its appointments—vast clawfoot tub, antique marble sink, mirrors trimmed with acres of baroque gilt, a chandelier that might have been hijacked from Buckingham Palace. One not directly under the other since the dark bog in the hall fourteen feet from the front door, while the upstairs bathroom flush with the front wall and flooded by light from a window. *Hers* at the top, *his* next to the foot of the hallway stairs, rooms separated, you could say, by the stair's angle of descent. He knows precisely how this small house's parts relate to one another because he'd gutted it, reframed and rebuilt it, sawing, sanding, hammering, measuring, painting from top to bottom, his project the three summers they had owned this place before he retired, as her project, after they've settled in for good, seems to be becoming the Queen of England, he'd snicker to Ralph if he ever gave anyone his honest opinion about this retirement business, this selling his big suburban home and moving further out to the country business, pissing in separate toilets, sleeping in separate beds. Since he'd made this house tight as a drum and

knows to the inch both the horizontal and vertical distance between upper and lower bathrooms, he wonders why he worries
when he's plopped down to take a crap and hears her bathroom
door click shut, worries a scalding flood of urine or her shit in
cast iron blocks will come crashing down on his head.

Clandestino

Her old friend opened a bar, *Clandestino*, on Canal Street on the lower east side. What gift to celebrate his good fortune. Maybe some pussy. But his new wife might not appreciate that. A threesome, maybe. Stoppit. She hates the nasty drift of her thoughts. Demeaning. Herself and everybody else in the world demeaned. Me, me, me. Always about me. First person even on the list of people I don't like. Demeaning myself. A nothing bitch. Going nowhere. Just pussy on the hoof to give away. Not sure half the time anybody wants it. *Biff-bam. Thank you, ma'am.* Gone. Out the door. Bye-bye, birdie. Maybe that's what he should have named his bar. *Biff-Bam's.* What's up with the *Clandestino* shit. He's no Italian. An Indian, maybe. Of the original American sneaky redskin variety. An Indian-giver. I give you my heart, he said in ancient times. Then took it back. Same ole, same ole. Need some space, Baby… need a little time to get my head together, he said, and promised to return with his heart, her heart in his grubby hands. Right. And here I sit, still waiting. Good thing I didn't hold my breath. Or maybe I should have. Held my breath like I'm holding it now to keep from bawling. If I'd held my breath, I'd be long gone and wouldn't be worrying about some stupid gift. Just wrap up my dead body and send it and wouldn't that be a nice surprise for him to open.

Kristol Ball

Money not her problem. Anything money could buy as close as her cell phone or already arranged by her staff for regular delivery. If it wasn't money anymore, what was it. Her problem of the moment Sniffy Poo (*Sniffy Poop*, when she said his name to herself) one of her rap acts who wanted to initiate a boycott of Kristol champagne because according to Sniffy a top Kristol exec had dissed the gangster element for bringing unwholesome associations to his company's product, thereby dissing Sniffy and his crew who very publicly guzzle Kristol like they'd guzzled Kool-Aid in the hood back in the day. She'd phoned the exec, who by coincidence, she knew from a Kristol floated six days together on a private Aegean island, and he claimed he'd been misquoted, but of course would apologize publicly, then laughed, ha-ha, and said, No. Tell Mr. Sniffy to bring it on. The only bad publicity is no publicity. Ha-ha. That part of the call cool. What wasn't okay, no mention of their hot island week. Through silk she squeezes flesh drifted to her waist. Shit. For half a minute wonders if she's lost her figure. And worse, thinks of the sacrifices required to get it back.

Her fine body next to Dave's had made them the foxiest chocolate couple on campus. The girls nicknamed Dave *The Body*, giggled when he passed. She'd loved that big nappyhead boy/man. Nobody else ever afterwards, nobody else even close. Loved him most maybe the day of the demonstration, the day before the night College Hall firebombed and Dave disappeared. So tall and proud haranguing the crowd, pledging to sacrifice body and soul to the revolution. In a corner of the lawn under a big tree with her light, bright AKA sisters, everybody cracked up when one of them shouted, "No, no. Not the body, Dave. Please don't give up that Body."

Where's Dave now. Abroad. Jail. Dead. Years without even a rumor. What did we think we were doing back then. What did we want. Did anybody know. Then. Now. One damned thing she's certain of. They weren't marching and demonstrating so Sniffy Poop could snort coke and swim in Kristol without getting his feelings hurt.

At the bottom of her letter to Sniffy, after encouraging the boycott and promising eternal solidarity, she signs her famous name and prints by hand the postscript: Stay in the struggle, Dog.

Answering Service

Now I'll call my dad. But I can't. He's dead. The thought *now I'll call my dad* coming naturally, faster than the speed of light before I could censure it or laugh or cry at the unthinking thought of phoning my father, dead now for six years, the thought coming because I'd just hung up after talking with my mom and the thought mize well call old pops since I'm on the phone anyway and it's been a while since we last talked so I'll call daddy even though it's never easy talking with him, that thought comes naturally you see because I've done my calling in spurts or in a serial fashion, you could say, for many years now, extended sessions of one call after another, maybe kicked off by one call I desire to make or one I must make and since I've got it going, in a groove or stuck, you might say, and the phone sits there, no excuse, ready again if I'm ready, I go on and make a bunch of calls until, forgive the dumb pun, I'm off the hook. I've just hung up after talking to my mom who at the moment is alive but very, very ill. And so am I. Alive. That's the thing about the phone, isn't it. When you call, there's a chance you'll get an answer. Life continues. Yours. Someone else's. Not always. These days even if you do get an answer it's likely to be a machine and very likely a machine's the last thing you want to hear. Machines aren't alive and they can make you wonder if you are. But a phone call's a chance, at least, of talking to someone alive besides yourself. Unless like my father the someone you call's dead. Then there's no chance. Unless you get their machine.

Bedtime Story

Strip, my father repeated, the gun, those terrible blue eyes trained on us again.

We're trapped—the whole family locked inside the glass-walled room. Nowhere to run. No place to hide.

Strip. And this time we do. Flinging off clothes as fast as we can. Andrew's dead on the floor. The hole my father, his grand-father, shot in his chest gushing blood.

You believe me now, don't you. Your fault I had to shoot to prove I mean business. Good riddance anyway. Andrew was worthless. A parasite. Cruel and craven. Dangerous. He's bet-ter off dead. Maybe the others will turn out a bit better, though I doubt it. But I won't shoot another one as long as you do exactly as I say. Strip and get it on.

You. You children stop squalling and turn your backs. Face the wall and don't turn around till you're told. You saw what happened to your bad big brother.

Do as he says, kids. Please. Please, kids. Turn around and don't be frightened. He won't hurt us, won't hurt you. He loves you. He's your grandfather.

I'll do what I have to do. Just shut the fuck up and get it on with her. I'm bored already.

How can you do this. Why are you doing this.

Whine. Whine. Whine. I gave you the power to ask questions because I enjoy the power of not answering.

Please stop this. Please.

I've always been curious about flesh. How flesh makes flesh. How flesh dies. What it is when it's not flesh and not dead. This time I'm going to watch. My self inside of you inside of her dying and being born into another being not you who becomes me and creates another you who creates me. Or something like that. My turn to be the criminal fleeing the scene of the crime. I'll get it right one of these times. Or try and try again. Now mount her. The children are getting cold and hungry. It's past their bedtime. We don't have all the time in the world.

Woman in Seascape

Beside a clump of huge boulders at the end of a densely wooded footpath that twists down steeply from the road to the beach, she sunbathes every clear day and some that aren't. One cloud-covered, blustery afternoon, tide swollen so water's less than ten yards away, she stands there staring at the sea, small breasts bare, brazen, as if daring the waves to roar up and finish her. On sun-drenched days flopped on her belly, flesh harshly browned, she appears more rather than less naked with one black string around her waist, another bisecting her plump buttocks. Definitely not young. Certainly not anybody's idea of a *femme fatale*. Even with those sad eyes and dark hood of hair, she's plain at best, if you scrutinize her aging features. Not a woman to be jealous of. Her man's eyes never drawn to the woman beside the rocks. Any man would find the uninvited neighbor far less attractive than she is, not worth a second glance, though she herself can't help studying and evaluating the solitary woman who sooner or later, inevitably it seems, occupies the spot next to the big rocks close by their favorite spot, the same nearly nude, long-haired woman, never addressed, never speaking, always alone on a huge white towel spread out on the sand, alone hour after hour baking in the sun, desperately alone it seems, desperation projected by the woman's posture, her silence, staring at the water for endless hours alone, *I'm alone* she hears the sound of the woman saying, *I'm alone, alone*, gray noise constant as moaning wind and water while she imagines lives for her, chilling, secret, soap opera traumas. When her man disappears, her impossibly tall, dark and handsome man, her impossibly smart, funny, loyal lover goes away like all the others and doesn't return, evaporating *poof* in thin air like a dream, she can't blame the woman who sets up lonely shop each day next to theirs. No. In fact she senses a sort of sisterhood or sistership, bitter enough, yes, but enough of it anyway to assume her place beside the massive stones and stare longingly at the sea, wondering for hours on end what the true story might be, looking for herself out there beyond the dazzle of horizon, looking for herself lying alone a few yards away, looking back.

Dear Madonna

This is my first letter to a famous person and I'm not sure about protocol. Am I presuming too much familiarity by addressing my letter to your first name, Madonna. If so, please forgive me because I know only one name for you. Do you have a last name. Or maybe Madonna is your family name. I've read the truly famous require only one name—like Jesus. So maybe addressing you as Madonna is a compliment, a tribute to your celebrity. I can't think of many women in history who have single name recognition. *Joan* needs *of Arc*. *Catherine* needs *the Great*. Anyway, since Madonna is the only name of yours I know, I'm wasting your time and mine with this protocol business. I've also read one doesn't need to put an address on a letter to a world famous person. The post office understands where his (*her* rarely, if ever) mail should be delivered. Like Santa and the President. But the President doesn't count exactly, does he (no *she* yet, maybe you should run, Madonna) because for instance the post office would be puzzled by an envelope with only *George* written on it, unless it also said former President of the United States and, well, that's clearly more than a single name. But that, Madonna (I feel more at ease already calling you Madonna after writing so much to you, if you've read this far, Madonna) is not what I started out to say, the point I wanted to make is that maybe you're more famous Madonna than the President, although a letter addressed to Obama might reach the present President, but he's busier than his predecessor, George, so I doubt very much he would have time to read a letter from me. Besides, Presidents are dangerous people. I wouldn't ever feel comfortable being on a single name basis with one. What would I write to him (or her) anyway, especially since he probably wouldn't open my letter. Maybe I should write: *Make Love not War*, a famous slogan from a bygone era when I was lots younger. And now that cat's out the bag, yes Madonna, I must admit I'm quite a bit older than you. I also might as well confess, if you've read this far and haven't guessed, this is a love letter, pure and simple, Madonna. When I read of your intention to adopt another child, I realized you, too, must be suffering a void in your emotional life. Given your fabled unconventionality and courageous trailblazing, why attempt to fill your void in such an unoriginal fashion. Adopt an old man instead. What could a smelly, squalling baby do for you, Madonna, that an old man couldn't do better. Adopt me, Madonna. I could furnish you a thousand convincing reasons, make a thousand promises in this letter, but I'm afraid you won't read them. But just think, Madonna, if you adopted me you could take my name and nobody (including love-sick letters like this one) would know how to find you.

Morning After

I think I'm going to stop listening. I think I don't want to hear anymore. I have a headache. The coffee isn't working. Next glass asks me to wash it, I'm smashing on the floor, crushing under my bare heel. Whose wedding is this anyway. Whose mother on the bier with a tiny gold cross just below the deep hollow of her throat. I think I was dancing. First thing I remember saying no this morning to the man who knocked quiet as a mouse then asks me to go fishing. Is this the same sky more or less out the window that was black last night, a home to stars while loons barked at the moon and I lost my virginity to a Kosher pickle. I keep getting busy signals. Everybody must be talking to everybody else. I take some satisfaction from the fact that when my head goes *pop*, nobody will hear it. Not even me.

New Work

There are pages there called new work I keep turning to find nothing there are pages called new work there I keep turning to find nothing new there is work there called new I keep finding turning to nothing new there I keep turning to nothing there are pages turning to nothing there I keep turning to find new work there turning to nothing called new work I keep turning pages to find.

Pierced

I beg her to tattoo the world on my chest. The first prick of the first needle excruciating. I scream. Can't help myself. Instantly ashamed because the tattoo my idea and I'd been warned, hadn't I, but insisted anyway and still a million million pricks to go and already I'm hollering and pissing my pants, quivering like a worm on the table. Besides, until the tattoo finished, no one exists to hear my cries, so shut the fuck up I snarl at myself and grit my teeth as her steady hand burns the world into my flesh. Light first, then darkness and bleeding colors to divide sky from earth from water, to shape land masses, mountains, to form the green fleece of vegetation that feeds and hides creatures who must die to feed plants and soil. After what feels like an eternity or like a flash faster than the speed of light beaming me from a painless universe to a universe consisting purely of pain, precisely that slowly and quickly, her cool shadow hovering over me while she works, peels away. Another scream erupts, but not mine this time and not loud, only the coarse Velcro rip of her disengaging and leaving.

Finished, I implore. No more. No more world. It's finished now, real now, isn't it, I plead. A dumb question. Who do I think will answer. She's gone. No answer forthcoming from the darkness she vacated nor from the tattoo she's sewn inside my chest.

Absolutely Perfect

Does Adam watch Eve as attentively as I watch you each morning, tracking every minute adjustment of Eve's body as she sits drinking her coffee and reading. Why would he. Eve's naked. Adam will never see more or less of her. Eve exposes nothing she's worried about covering or uncovering. Each glimpse of Eve absolutely perfect in Adam's eyes as the next. The last. What else could he be looking for. Beyond naked. Beyond perfect. Eve happy Adam watches. Adam happy watching Eve's unchanging perfection. If he isn't, how would she know, unless he risks telling her, and why would he risk making both of them unhappy.

I wonder how Eve would look to Adam if she, like you, turned up in a bikini each morning to stretch out on her lawn chair. How would Adam in a bikini look to her. What causes me to think there are white plastic recliners in the Garden of Eden just because we have them in ours. Would Eve own bikinis and sheer, silky wraps like yours. Would Adam own a swim suit. Would Eve look more naked or less naked wearing nothing except your small, round spectacles perched on her nose. Would such a trivial detail unleash fiery erotic possibilities. Eve wouldn't own eyeglasses, would she. Adam and Eve not middle-aged like us with eyes that require correction. Age irrelevant as bikinis and lawn chairs in Eden.

Naked under one of your graceful, revealing wraps, while she reads and sips coffee Adam brews for them every morning, is Eve certain her privacy's intact. Or does she spy on Adam's eyes like you spy on mine. Like mine spy on you. Does Adam worry his eyes are missing something. Does Eve worry she'll find something missing in Adam's eyes. Are both worried about other eyes always watching that miss nothing.

My guess is that Adam and Eve are spared such cumbersome concerns. Each captive of the Garden allowed to dream a separate garden with separate rules to shield them from pain and danger, separate rules, for instance, governing the placement of fig leaves and gazes. And dream different dreams of escape. Could it be any other way in a perfect garden forever. My dream each morning you forget a wrap or forget there's no bikini beneath it, forget my eyes. And yours.

Ghetto

The King's dead. He lifts his wet son from the crib. A quiet, quiet baby, soaked and he protests not. No outcry yesterday when a waterbug prowled the crib, settled on his fat, beige cheek. His son's mother the one who hollers when she discovers the huge black insect. Flicks it off. Snatches up her baby and screams in fear, for help, for the father to kill or shoo or rescue, a blood curdling cry if ever he'd heard one, him racing naked from bed to the alcove they called the baby's room to find her backed against the wall furthest from the crib, clutching their son to her breast, her face aged a hundred years since he'd switched off the bed lamp that night. How could the baby still be so young, so quiet in the arms of this ancient woman who sobs, *Out of here...please... we've got to get out of here.* Yesterday. Scared woman with baby clamped to her bosom, bareass man gawking at the monster in the crib. A scene from a movie or book, familiar with a kind of déjà vu authority. A frozen moment that waits for him to renew their acquaintance. Yesterday. The day they shot King in Memphis. Just yesterday, at this same early morning hour, he'd run here naked, summoned by a scream yanking him from the usual tired conversation with himself, *C'mon boy. Move your sorry black ass, boy.* Tired before he rolls out of bed, tired of waking up in the same dead-end place where he'd dropped off to sleep.

Still dark outside yesterday when he'd run here and scooped the beetle from the crib in a mitt of Pamper, lucky to grab a wet not shitty one from the waste basket on the changing table. With all his might he'd squeezed the thick wad, hoping to hear a nasty pop. Twice he slammed it down on the dresser top under the hard meat of his hand, then hurled it to the floor, stomping, grinding white plastic and paper flat under his bare heel. Just yesterday. The baby quiet through the whole silly business. Quiet this morning twenty-four hours later. Lifted wet from his crib. What does his son remember about yesterday. What will he tell him. *The King's dead.*

A Story About Color for Children Born With Many

(for Q, my granddaughter)

Do you ever wonder what color you are, Q. No word for your color, Sweetheart. Your color is a story not a word. Many, many stories. Before you accept anybody's word for your color, look in the mirror. Looking is listening because what you will see in the mirror are stories voices inside you tell.

But the voices can't begin a story—can't say *green girl in the mirror* or say *black girl* or say *brown girl* or say *red girl*—without words. A voice can't even say *girl* without words. A story needs words, and words need a language like French or Arabic or English or Chinese or Chimpanzee, so you can understand what others mean when they say a word.

Imagine the baby you were twelve years ago, Q. A less than one year old searching for her color in a mirror. Without language, without words, what would she see. Would she just stare and stare silently. Or maybe get bored and make up her own ga-ga-ga language. If she has no word for *bored*, could she get *bored* or just keep on quietly staring, you know, like dogs and cats stare forever, unless hunger or fright or sleep steal her eyes from the mirror because the strongest feelings don't need words to get us moving, do they.

Maybe the cute baby would stare into the mirror until someone calls her. But how would she know someone's calling her if she doesn't learn a language people use when they want her or

95

don't want her or want to say something about her, like the name of her color.

No girl—certainly not the one in this story who's sort of like you, Q—wants to stare forever or be silent forever or alone forever, so she learns words like *happy*, Q, or like *shoe, tree*, or words for a rainbow of colors. And if she's quick and smart like you, she makes words into stories about what she thinks and feels and sees. Makes up her own stories about her many colors in the mirror. Stories that help her live happily ever after.

The Puzzle for Puzzling's Sake Meaning Not a Goddamn Thing

There's a certain fashionable method, quite overbearingly fashionable really, of constructing narrative—stories, films, lives, wars—that drives me wild. Wildly angry like I get at the conclusion of an O'Henryesque *surprise! surprise!* ending story when the final piece falls into place and all the rigamarole of the story's preceding bill of particulars that's been so painstakingly delivered to consume my attention turns out to be a cheap trick, *gotcha,* sort of like strip tease, with not even any golden-fleeced genitalia behind the last transparent wisp of cover-up. The formula for achieving these fashionable constructions which drive me to distraction is simple. Any apprentice serial killer knows the drill. You chop up a perfectly ordinary body. One as commonplace, arbitrary, and unappealingly familiar as your own body will do. Then deposit the pieces in various sites—the more exotic or unexpected the locales, the better. When discovered, each morsel—finger, spleen, thigh—will elicit shock, disgust, fear. A scrambled sequence of body parts appearing one by one on the screen far more provocative than the whole body ever could manage, traipsing past on its own. Ear. Heart. Appendix. The audience gasps, Oh shit. My god. What unimaginable horror is unfolding. What manner of horrible beast is responsible. This in spite of the fact that the audience knows perfectly well that a large, undistinguished piece of meat chopped into smaller bits, remains, after all is said and done, the same ole undistinguished meat. And so what.

But someone's been murdered and mutilated, you assert. A once live body cut up into dead body parts isn't exactly a minor event, you insist. Then to clinch your argument for patronizing this form of entertainment , you add, Afterall, the victim could be Cousin Bob or Aunt Mary, right.

My reply: Ain't no Aunt Mary or Cousin Bob. No such relatives in my family. Nor yours. No live toads nor once upon a time live dead body parts in those imaginary gardens. Only mannequins. Dummies. Clones. A silicone breast in the shape of a person chopped up into little pieces. It drives me wild. All the king's horses, all the king's men putting nothing whatsoever back together again.

Condemned

I don't like him. But one thing you could say for the motherfucker. He got perfect teeth. Perfect. They sit shiny and white and perfect in a little silver tray on his big desk and I can't help agreeing with what I'd always heard everybody say. Those teeth sure nuff impressive. I'm in his office today because this is my ninth death sentence and none of the previous eight had been delivered with anything approaching the speed and efficiency of this one. Perfect. Like the teeth.

Good morning, Mr. Mayor. I'd like to take this opportunity to thank you and your administration for how expeditiously youall handled my case.

Contrary to popular opinion, we do our honest best here. Our very best.

Well, I for one wish to express my profoundest gratitude, Mr. Mayor. When I woke up this morning, thought to myself, why not tip on by the Mayor's office and thank him in person. See if he has any message he'd like me to carry to folks on the other side.

I appreciate your sentiments and your offer. Just tell the folks on the other side that things are never what they seem. No matter how pretty a few of us appear to be sitting, there are troubling issues, dangerous issues threatening all citizens. Somebody must perform the dirty work of keeping these issues in check, and somebody has to suffer when we do our work well.

Word, Mr. Mayor. I'll be sure to tell everybody over yonder just what you say.

Thank you. I've always had a good feeling about you. Even after I was advised you'd committed heinous crimes. I can tell by your willingness to be an emissary that your heart's in the right place. *Auf weidersehen*, my friend.

A little *quid pro quo*, if you please, Mr. Mayor. Tell everybody on this side I said, *Hi* and *Bye*. Tell them life ain't fair, but the moral arc of the universe curves slowly towards justice. Tell them I do my best under the circumstances, Mr. Mayor. Just like you do your best. Tell them you'd get my vote if I had one, and tell them voting for you is like voting for me. *A demain*, my man. And don't let nobody tell you, Mr. Mayor, you ain't got some dynamite teeth.

Crossover

No love in him, just flattery, deception, relentless discipline, ruthlessness and patience till he stole her love and she allowed him to use his appliances on her, the boxful of brightly colored toys pulled from under his bed, toys to plug into her, vibrate, tickle, squeeze, stretch places she was shocked to hear him say the nasty names of out loud, names that confirmed the existence of those places, amazed that any decent man would even mention those troublesome sites, let alone express an interest in going there, his interest offending her, confusing her, disgusting her slightly after he kissed her the first time there or there, as if he possessed a natural right and she possessed no rights. She grew worried, depressed, resigned finally after his constant pleading and nagging made such trespassing routine, not exactly aware finally of her capitulation, when or where or why, until the day it dawned on her those places had been the prize he'd been seeking from the start, and she'd been duped, inch by inch, until he achieved her total submission and yes, humiliation, by what his toys performed, by what he'd done and she allowed him to do to her body, and worse, what she'd done to her mind, convincing herself that it wasn't about the fun, expensive gifts he sugar-daddied her, telling herself no, no, no way, it's not that stuff, no, it was love, her will to save him, redeem his good parts in spite of his dangerous, ugly parts, love tempting her, not the surprises he handed out as if he owned the world, love, wasn't it love, tempting her to take a chance, take his hand in hers and flee, naked as Eve and Adam, from her innocence into the promised land of his pleasure.

Showtime

Old raggedy black man always there chewing on his fingers in the shadowy, below-ground pit outside the basement door of the next to last apartment building from the corner. At first she believes he's sadly, savagely mad. Scrunched in smelly darkness under the stone steps like some creepy sideshow cannibal gnawing his own flesh. She hated the burlesque insult of his eyeballs pinwheeling, two thick fingers fed like a juicy hot dog to his grinning mouth, the snake tongue licking his lips. Wondered if every female passerby treated to the same trick. The man seemed to never sleep. Eyes never closed, never lost in space. They stared unblinking, waiting for her each time. Eyes hollering at her. She hears them whether she looks or not, and she can't help herself, catches herself looking every morning until gradually she understood a sequence of exactly repeated gestures preceded his final, grotesque finger gobbling. First two fingers scissoring mimicked her thin brown legs trot, trot, clickety-click, high heels stabbing the broken pavement. His sash-shaying wrist the sway of African print dresses or flounce of a tailored suit's mini-skirt or hips in hip-hugger slacks topped by a silky blouse, a fashion show every morning on her way downtown to a good job. She had no idea how he added audio to the video of his pantomime, but she could hear it playing plain as day. If she was honest with herself, she would have to admit she danced to the cadence of his words some mornings or admit the words rhythming her steps so deep inside her they might or might not be his, might be, even though she'd be the last person on earth to admit it, words she sang to herself. *Where you think you going little mama wit them fine sugar mama babycakes girl. Ummm. Ummm. Them down-town folks gon eat you up, child. Mmmm—Ummm. Eat you alive. Lick up every bit of your chocolate pudding and sweet meat just like you see me working all the grit and gristle and grease off dis bone.*

More or Less

He returns from Kinko's with many copies of himself. At first I thought it was funny. Pleased by the prospect of an inexhaustible supply of fresh lovers. Then I panicked. Which one of the identical copies the original. How would I ever know. What if none of them the original. Where is it, then. Did he forget it on the screen under the lid of the copy machine for the next customer to find. Maybe he stashed it somewhere. Hidden from me on purpose. Maybe he's deposited the original in somebody else's hands. Whose hands. Why. Why is he confusing me. Which one is him. All these smiling copies one after another after another, impossible to tell apart. Why is he doing this to me. I attack. Ripping, shredding the stack, waiting for one to holler, hoping one will bleed.

Review

You don't have to be very smart to write a review of a book of short stories. All you need to say is that some stories in the book are better than others. Everybody agrees that's the way it works with collections of short stories. It's not necessary to read the stories, just scan the table of contents and cite in your review the title of one story you say you like and one you don't like. This specificity will impress the readers of your review, establish your credibility and seriousness. Don't stress yourself selecting which title to admire or pan since almost none of your readers will ever read any of the stories you're reviewing. Readers will be less favorably disposed towards your review if you say all the stories in the collection suck or all the stories are great because your reading, based upon their previous experience of reading or not reading books of stories and reading or not reading reviews of books of stories and based upon their previous experience of life in general which is, afterall, what stories are about, will have concluded that some things are better than other things and this being the case, for stories as well, why stir up readers by suggesting you think your experience of reading stories or your experience of life in general is different than your reader's experience and maybe you believe you're smarter than they are, whereas everybody knows you don't need to be born all that smart to write a review of a book of stories or write the stories either.

Fall

She happens to be glancing at him when he lets go the handle bar of his piled high shopping cart and turns his head fast like somebody's called his name over his shoulder—lets go and turns and takes a quick step in the opposite direction he had been pushing the cart—a step too fast for an old man—where's he think he's going in such a big hurry—then clearly not a step—he's falling—falling and dead before he hits the pavement – not catching hisself—falling chin first—face all twisted up sideways on the pavement—snaggleteeth in the wrong place—and she's surprised by none of this—goes to him—kneels—not surprised by stink almost suffocating her—yes, yes, like once long ago when she sneaked up under her rocking chair great-granny's long black dress—not surprised he's not finished shitting and pissing hisself—though one wide-open eye saying dead, dead, dead—not surprised he shudders and one last twitch lifts a foot clean off the pavement—not surprised blood and nastiness leak down his chin—been here, done this—her turn soon—dying in broad daylight out in the street—that hood over her head of bad, sweet smell—she pats his old, dead shoulder, says, So long, Mister, Sorry Mister—unsurprised till he answers, Hush child. Everything gon be alright.

Art After Auschwitz

In the old, blurred, black and white photo he chanced upon of naked women running—droves and droves of women racing through the frame—why did he look for a pretty one in the crowd, a pretty face and trim figure, look, in other words he thought, with the innocent, reasonable eyes of a boy desiring life not death, desiring love to save himself and save one at least of these running women, snatching her from doom, insisting on the impossible possibility of love, even there in that old terrible place, one woman's hand grasped, him holding his ground, even at the risk of being swept away in a mass of panicked, driven flesh, pale melting flesh confirmed as female by dark fists of hair between the legs, faint arcs of breast, dark hatching of eye and nose, dark blot of mouths, O-shaped, screaming perhaps in the dash through frigid air, screams silenced by a camera watching, listening, catching white confusion of ghosts streaming across white Polish turf that may be contoured by forlorn drifts of snow or flat as a sheet of ice, it's difficult for a viewer to distinguish exactly what's what since most of the ungrained enveloping whiteness is a single tone, most of the darkness black holes in this shot somebody snapped, some visitor perhaps stunned by a sudden wave of shrieking, shivering, bareass women or perhaps an official photographer on duty too long carelessly leaves the shutter open too long so we see a stampede, unfocused except for deepest shadows, fiery licks of incandescence. Why did he search the picture for hints of attractiveness, for loveliness. Is beauty under the circumstances of the photo that much more impressive, undeniable, unquenchable, beyond desire, beyond atrocity and obscenity, beauty consecrated, proved by the special one he saves, her fingers gripped in his, *How could I let you get away,* the boy sings to himself, to her, imitating the Manhattan's high tenor lead, smiling, peering at her around a black border of guards whose thick hats and thick columns of overcoat artfully crop one edge of the scene or is the composition accidental, an unavoidable accident as he often feels himself to be, black dots and white dots refusing to align themselves symmetrically, harmoniously, or does love free him outside the frame, free to grope for design, proportion, meaning in a chaos of barely discernible limbs, torsos, shaved heads, an accidental witness of an accident, like a trespassing camera slapped out of someone's hands that accounts for the dizzying, bizarrely askew perspective of this blurry snapshot of running women that stretches across two pages, an oblique line of women who occupy a disintegrating strip of partial intelligibility exploding between unintelligibilities of obliterating light above and below what little the viewer's able to see of them, as if a falling machine could blink or hiccup or wince once before it strikes the frozen ground or shudder on impact and helplessly engrave one memory plate within itself with this death rattle image, and he's considering all this—silence, cold, moans, swirling snow, the unmistakable, unshameable urge or intent of his gaze—until overwhelmed, he sees not himself staring, sees another boy just like him long before he's blinded by a rush of doomed women, sees for the first time or rather remembers when he noticed for the first time, squeezed into a narrow band that ran just below the ceiling of an elementary school classroom where lucky brown American kids like him were taught French grammar a thousand years ago, sees the still-born horror of motion arrested furiously, arrested motion rendered to unnatural clarity in a decorative plaster frieze of running horses straddled by bare-thighed Roman warriors way too big for their mounts, a pile-up of terrified, rearing horses, bulging eyes and nostrils, flayed muscles and bones exposed in stark relief, imploding haunches, stiff flags of bobbed tail, jack-o-lantern grimaces of bared teeth, stone-fingered claws of riders who grip rippling manes and Sabine women's hair.

Now You See It

You come to a space on the page and can't read further because in this space resides everything the writer does not know, pretends to know, cannot know – the face of a god, for instance, the emptiness and fullness of time, perfect silence, voices of the dead returning—all crammed clamoring into this white space between two words or space dividing blocks of print on a page, as if the unnameable, unimaginable can be put on hold in a space the writer may have chosen to leave blank in order to suggest a plan or design or transition or simply provide a rest stop for pilgrims in the story before they pick up their burdens again and continue their journey, but whatever the writer's intent, the space suddenly uncrossable, too much missing, too much erased, you falter, unclear why you've read this far, the space yawns wider and wider and sucks in the whole world, including the writer's dream dreamed up to fashion a story, to fashion a space within the story for you, your dreams, and there's no going forward, no going back, nothing survives the space, no words, no page, no safe passage the writer promised through roaring silence that closes like the sea over heads of creatures who cannot swim, the story gone before the writer's next word.

First Love Suite

I.

On a rainy day with nothing better to do three guys sit around telling stories of first loves. The first two stories of first love never happen. What you mean, *first love*, man. First time I copped some pussy, you mean, the first guy wonders aloud. The second guy smiles, sighs, closes his eyes like he's died and gone to whatever heaven on earth he roamed wit his first love, leaving the other two guys far behind, neither one very interested in the second guy's reverie anyway, one guy because he's still scratching his head, trying to figure out what constitutes a first love, and the other guy disinclined to follow very far into the enchanted forest of the second guy's daydream which might be a bit like watching the second stalled storyteller masturbate, not an alluring activity to consume time even on a rainy day, he thinks, unless it's him, himself getting off, which he isn't, doesn't while he contemplates two failed story telling attempts and the prospect of his own failure since what else could he say or anyone say that wouldn't be, more or less, a repeat of the stories untold so far, the first one being not having a fucking idea what a first love is, and the second being consumed by dropping off an edge and plummeting arms flailing towards a bottom, to which there is no bottom, thus how or why would you attempt to tell another guy or two guys in this case, your story if you're busy falling, your mouth full of hollering or screaming and a sweet, juicy tongue you've been searching for, waiting for, dreaming of for years, root, root, rooty-toot-toot all up in your gums and tickling your sinus passages and tonsils from the wet pink inside.

II.

Three little pickininnies jumping on the bed / One fell off and the other two said / Ha-ha / We see your hiney / All black and shiny. But instead of acting the fool, I take my story telling turn seriously.

Once upon a time on a day besieged by rain heavy and gray as the rain today keeping us indoors, nagging, hassling each other with taunts of story, boasts of story, story as withholding, story as ache, as mule, as mirror, story the ten counts separating us before we turn and fire story at each other, once upon a time on a day that could be this one, sheets of rain are striking my face, and I cannot imagine why the girl I met here on the beach yesterday isn't here now where we both promised we'd be, cross our hearts and hope to die, no matter what.

It's the summer of 1960. An Atlantic City, New Jersey beach. A city, believe it or not, I'll return to about thirty years later accompanying Mr. Jesse Jackson who's running for first black President of the United States. Now I'm alone. Barely twenty years old. Unable to imagine another lifetime for myself longer than the life already lived. And not tempted to try. The future considered only to reassure myself I have one coming. At this present moment things about as dark and final as they get. Night. Rain still pouring as it's poured all day. Sand rutted by mammoth earthworm trails of erosion wriggling towards the ocean. The sea, unfamiliar to an inland Pittsburgh boy like me, a huge wetness churning noisy as a busy laundromat. Flashes of white flop and blink way out there in the black wet like glimpses of soapy sheets tumbling through discs of window in washing machine doors. If you put your bare feet in the sea. I'd discovered yesterday, sea water sneaks up your ankles and wiggles down again, ticklish like wool socks pulled off, and while you're distracted by the feeling of your naked ankles being undressed, your whole body gets sucked down, toes first, then the thick lumps of heel because puddles empty and fill under them, water swims through your wiggling toes with the greatest of ease, all of you sucked down, sinking into a dark, wet hole, the dead weight of your body spinning fast like the earth spins because sneaky gravity's always there sucking you down , heavier and heavier as you wait at night in a strange city, by a strange ocean, looking for a strange, no, a beautiful, very, very beautiful girl, I'm sure, no doubt about it, a beautiful girl who promised yesterday to meet me here but nowhere now to be seen

Where is she. Where's anyone go the moment you take your eye off them.

Meanwhile, here I am on the beach digging a hole to bury myself or having one excavated for me in damp sand by a little round-butted, wasp-waisted, 17 or 18 year old nappy head brown girl whose unbearable absence at this moment is like having my skin pulled off and the rawness salted and then whipped because I can't run, can't hide. Wet. Burning. I'm here. She's not. How could she lie to me. Lying with the same sweet, lips I kissed wetly, lips she pecked, dry and scratchy everywhere on my bare skin which no one has ever accomplished as perfectly before or since, gently as the finest sandpaper final rub of the balsa wood fuselages I'd carve for my model planes before I'd paint them and apply the decals—stars, swastikas, rising suns—which come in the kit. Yesterday on almost perhaps this exact same spot, ignoring crowds of sunbathers around us, we kissed numerous times, more than I could count, more than I can remember now or remembered then after the tipping point I do recall of 22, the last number I registered so the final total of kisses somewhere after that, between 23 and infinity. Twenty-two times at least let's say before a kind of swoon like when, they say, the sea washes in and takes everything away with it. Then I hear her voice as she hurries off. Gotta go to work now. Please. Please. Come back tomorrow night. I promise I'll be here. Don't forget me.

Thus her mermaid's song speaks or spoke. I can't commit to a verb tense and attach it to her, my first love, without swallowing the whole black, wet sea, without an agonizing death by drowning or fire. I can't tell you her weight, height, color of eyes, texture of skin, her name I can't remember or never learned, her clothes, gaze, smell gone so how can I confirm her presence or express her absence in this story of first love, guys, I'm telling no better than you guys told yours.

She doesn't return the next night—or next or next or next— no matter how long I stand getting wetter and wetter staring at the sea. Or I don't stand waiting on the beach long enough. Or maybe I'm still standing there and it's still raining and she knows better than to trust her heart to a fool who'd venture out in awful weather like this looking for love.

III.

I think stories are about holes in people's lives and every story
is a hole and the reason the hole for a grave is six feet deep is because once upon a time humans were buried vertical not horizontal and average height being what it was in those ancient days, a
hole six feet deep sufficed in almost every instance to disappear
with room to spare the person or former person with earth packed
around them so they stay erect, like in life, below ground, then a
small, decorative mound raised, sealing the hole in remembrance
of the dead person, making the dead person seem taller, like a god,
than six feet, the dirt crown a kind of precursor of tombstones
that come about later in history and grow monumental as larger
gods are worshipped. Increases in average human height necessi-
tated deeper vertical holes or slanting holes, until the living began
laying the dead flat on their backs in holes dug in a horizontal
direction, which became the prevailing custom and remains ours,
and though most people have forgotten why, we continue to sink
each grave to an old-time, nostalgic depth of six feet, except now,
today, with runaway overpopulation, there's a good argument
for upright burial again, dead people like in life jammed side by
side as in rush hour Tokyo subways or like pencils in my pencil
can or perhaps horizontal stacking, tight layer upon layer starting miles deep another idea, though the best idea, I believe, is fire,
very, very hot fire, better even than hi-tech ejaculations of bodies
into deep space which isn't as infinite as some pretend, just like
there aren't infinite spermacules in an average wad of semen—
though the numbers run to hundreds of thousands and over, I
think I read, in a good healthy discharge, meaning fewer eggs

get fertilized than you'd guess—many called, few chosen—as the oldest love story goes, and many a childless woman weeps away her child-bearing years, and many years afterward as if there's infinite room for grief in the hole of bygone years.

Wolves

He made up the story because...because he could, and when the people around him began to understand his story wasn't true, when he desperately needed someone to believe him and despaired of finding anyone who would, except his mother maybe, and she'd been dead for years, those truths, plus the fact of his mother herself as a lost, unimpeachable truth among very few truths he'd convinced himself he'd discovered and experienced, living, breathing truths he could honor, could share with someone else, except or despite these few truths, because they failed him or he failed them, his life had become a tissue of lies, generating daily more falsehoods, a deepening, darkening, fermenting slough infected at the core, an accelerating runaway train of illusion and self-delusion eradicating his power to distinguish true from plausible from possible from pure fantasy in the brew of his stories, even in this last straw, last ditch string of words, for instance, beginning how far back, back to the initial *He* at least that commences this wistful coming to terms, this accounting and cashing out gesture delivered with an urgency he truly feels this morning, through it's beyond him to be certain what he might feel tomorrow or how he'll feel when he reaches the end of this sentence he's scratching, quiet as breath in drumming early morning silence, silence that throbs loud as the heartbeat of someone imagined, someone you're wishing for who may never have existed, not there once upon a time to love, not here now to love, all he hears now the faint, dry scratch of yellow pencil against yellow pad, a sound as far as he can tell, for the moment anyway, he's not making up, not losing his place again in whatever it is he calls his life, his story, his words following on after another, erasing, consuming each other, ending like these.

Dog In My Eye

The dog sits in a corner of my eye dignified as a sphinx, mammoth sphinx paws carved from stone resting on the sill of a window opening into me and howls mournfully, burning and stinging my eye as if a pinprick of live ash has landed, this dog like a person on ice skates knifes around the white corner of my eyeball when I try to see it, my eyes blink-blink, blinking tears to dislodge this dog smaller than a flea and equally elusive, anonymous, invisible when I check in the mirror, but not gone, it still sits where it sits no clue how or why or where it goes when I try to see it, though I imagine for some reason or another it's a male creature spotted with muddy blotches of gray who's sitting in my eye, quieter now, no burn, a sting, tiny enough to trouble me about nothing in particular just enough so I'm remembering and losing precious sleep reviewing the usual suspects, every wound physical and metaphysical delivered by my life up to this very instant, trying to guess why a dog was sent to sit in a corner of my eye, disappearing when I rotate my gaze in its direction, returning at once when I stop looking for it, my awareness of its presence unceasing whether or not it goes away or never was there or may no longer be there, this dog dropping from the moon, from the corner of an eye of the lonely man who lives up there or arriving because the moon man's here in this room in a corner of the dog's eye searching for it.

Ralph Waldo Ellison

The snoring of two brown bodies inside an abandoned car rattles its cracked windshield. Rattling keeps the glass almost free of ice and turns into the shiver of a freight train within the dream of one of the teen-aged brothers bundled inside the jalopy in all the clothes he owns, shake, rattle, rolling boxcars the boy running away from Oklahoma will hear the final night of his life rattling on rails beneath the daybed in the living room of a New York City apartment rich with African masks, fabrics and carvings, the apartment he never leaves his last days, an apartment, a daybed become nightbed he can't escape except on the El rattling blocks away or memories of trains recorded in old jazz or blues licks on records or ancient nightmares, a boy shaken by teeth sunk deep in his tender neck, the boxcar he's hopped split open like a watermelon's pink belly by a booted foot, dozens of roachy black seeds scattering, a claw catching him by the scruff of his skull, a train at night in the distance passing by, the train he's been waiting for, listening for, he blows on his icy hands, hears the shivering car window, rattle of coffee perking, shadowy figures circled round a fire, posse of railroad bulls raiding the camp in the woods at dawn, bust up, burn, he's nabbed, pleads high ambitions and for some goddamn reason he never sorts out, the rednecks release him, maybe with smirks and a *keep this nigger running* pat on the ass he thinks he remembers telling it that way later to his wife he instructed absolutely, precisely how to do it so the coffee snaps him awake but doesn't panic him, so much to do he tells the men armed with state-issue cattle-prods and shotguns, so little time, the coffee should remind him but not abandon him, his icy hands glowing in the dark, his brother snoring, the Oklahoma City moon a frozen, pock-marked thing with a dangling, sticky-glue tongue that wags and drools, whips at warp-speed along invisible tracks chasing unwary colored boys, gobbling them up.

Cudjo After the Bombing and Fire in Philadelphia

On his first morning back after ten years on a Greek Island, after running and hiding for ten years, he's ready to confess now, confess his flight without feeling the need to take off running again, the scrufty turf of Clark Park bristling through his sandal's thin soles, the empty hoop court just ahead, a lover nodding, *Uh-huh, uh-huh* as if she had known all along he couldn't stay away, mouldy old brass Dickens behind him, still asleep on his stone throne with Little Nell below, still green and imploring, everywhere the flesh and blood of innocents borne here eight months ago by the fire's black smoke and ash, soaked into the soil by now, risen as dew and vapor then falling again as rain to feed grassy patches that survive here and there, rain igniting the perfume of clusters of tiny white flowers spattering short trees or tall bushes along the path above the hollow, wet and glistening, he thinks, spring, he thinks, his running, running steps almost silent behind him now, the park cool and quiet as shadows the victims cast, their abandoned clothing hidden beneath anything taller than a few inches.

Installation

At first I think it's a spill of ice cream, miraculously unmelted on the hot pavement. Rainbow of pistachio, lemon chiffon, strawberry, blueberry, chocolate raspberry ripple. Then I think it's a baby bird tumbled from its nest. After inspecting closer I see the bands of color too regular, too smooth for feathers and no recognizable birdy parts surviving—no eye, no yellow beak, no threads of leg or feet—in this lumpy little puddle of whatever, dropped from whatever great height it had fallen to get here under the Williamsburg bridge from wherever it had been before, and I'm curious and kneel and dare a taste from one quick, poked-in finger. Shit. Not roadkill. Not warmed-up Dairy Freeze either. It's shit some artist colored with bright stripes. A painted piece of shit. What will they think of next.

Vital

Unable to read another word he'd written, disbelieving every single word read so far, he lets the pages he'd struggled through flip slowly from under his thumb, thinking as he watches them fall of a bank teller priming bills, of a lane of naked scalp dividing the corn-rowed hair of a grand-niece fidgeting to scoot down from his knee.

Today, they are scanning his youngest sister's body to ascertain if cancer cells discovered in a hipbone have migrated to any vital organ. *Vital* his brother-in-law had said. Does *vital* mean alive or mean necessary for sustaining life, or both or either, he'd asked himself, listening yesterday to the stark recital by his sister's husband of bad news a surgeon had delivered. If vital could indeed signify either or both, then aren't all a person's organs, in one sense or the other, vital, and would that fact, if it's a fact, raise or lower his sister's chances of survival, he had wondered, but didn't interrupt with his questions. *Vital*. A prospect of loss beyond words and he'd welcomed the puzzle of a word. Couldn't wait to be alone with a dictionary looking up *vital*, afloat with all the other words in a calm sea of words while Sara sinks, perhaps gone already or gone soon as if she never existed, disappearing fast as streaming ghosts, one by one, claiming to be his memories of her.

He's ashamed as he recalls his response to the man married 30 years to Sara. Only ticking emptiness inside, no feelings, no words he could speak to break the silence between himself and a man whose features had suddenly become unfamiliar, silence ticking like one empty word following another and another printed on a page. Were human beings supposed to be equipped with an organ connecting them to other humans. Why doesn't mine work. *There*, he almost shouts aloud. There's the answer— known all along—to the question he chose not to ask his sister's husband. *No*. Not all organs vital. Yes, Some organs a person could survive without. Living proof dead inside him.

His book stillborn. Arriving dead out of him surely as his sisters and brothers born hollering out of the woman he called Mom. *Mom* his first word. Maybe his only vital word. *Mom* for all his 65 years on the planet, and *Mom* gone now, speeding away after the final page of many pages her years produced. The teeming book of his mother containing his brothers' and sisters' limp-along stories, grim, messy, more than enough drama to fill volumes he couldn't write, and now his, his what... story, new novel, a project he understood clearly better left unwritten, better leafed through in reverse, back to front, and erased word by word, and maybe during the process he might get lucky—if and when it's ever over, begun again, never started—and find the secret of its' wanting to live.

Afterlife

After she settles into the darkness, just inches from him, quiet as she makes herself so as not to disturb him, the earth shudders and cracks, the knee or hip he caresses to tell her don't worry, I'm not exactly asleep, is cold, yes, as cold as the cold sea, she says without a word, not breaking the silence they conspire to keep real, her moving quietly, so quietly, though she concedes the fact she's sneaking like a thief into his bed, snuggling closer, an arm, a thigh draped over him, the start of one of those puzzles two bodies nearly asleep try to figure out, two bodies desiring to occupy the same warm pocket of space with their not quite interlocking limbs and unforgiving knobs of bone, a puzzle they struggle to solve without keeping themselves awake while they solve it, but never quite manage, sooner or later, one or the other must turn away if either's going to steal a decent night's sleep, sleep a thing they can't do clamped together no matter how close their bodies come to working it out, embracing, drifting, melting, sleep eludes them like the secret she can't quite bring herself to share, *Remember, love,* he's thinking—loud enough to be heard, he hopes—remember the story you never finish—about the man catching you stealing in his store and blackmailing you—you never say what he forced you to do. I've been waiting for you to say and something keeps me asking, even now. You promise you'll tell me another day or say you can't remember, though once you admitted you recall every detail precisely and will never forget.

A long time ago, she'd say again if she could hear him again. I was very young, she'd say again. Or say, The whole business terrible. It hurts me. I don't want to remember.

He turns to wrap her nakedness tighter into his. The cold's deep, even her belly. His fingers locate the bump of tailbone. Press into the crease at the top of her haunches, imagining the cavity below, the promise of warmth hoarded in its emptiness, reassuring himself with the unlikelihood that nature would provide an opening into a space unless the space exists.

How old exactly were you when it happened. Though he asks nothing, sees nothing, hears nothing in the darkness, her reply, he's certain, is many many questions, her huge eyes punctuating each one, sea-green eyes threatening to disappear, to look away and maybe never returning.

Do you envy the power that man lorded over me. Would you enjoy watching. Where were you, my love. Why didn't you help me. Save me. What would you have done in my place. His. How old exactly are you now. Are you upset I've returned late from the concert. Do you wonder what Taj played. Are you sorry you missed it. Are you wondering where I've been, whose arms I grew cold in.

You're back

Of course I am. Where else would I be

Are you happy here

Yes. Are you

Now I am. Yes. This moment

It's late love, We should try and get some sleep

Will you ever say what happened in the back room of that man's stupid store

Taj played *Corinna, Corinna* your favorite once. Is it still. Don't answer. Hush now. Sleep my love

Will you

Yes. Right here beside you

Always

Yes

Paris Morning, Rue Blomet—
6:47 am—July 10, 2007

1, 2, 3, 4 birds flutter up and perch on top of a Paris apartment building. Birds the color of stains where the whitish, pillbox plain structure bleeds at its seams, corners, along the edge of its flat roof on which the birds stay just a few moments before dropping like stones past 5 or 6 upper stories then below treetops he can see from a window above the kitchen sink. The blank-walled, massive, squared unloveliness of the building squatting where it squats, the birds landing precisely when and where they land, staying precisely as long as they stay, tell time exactly as the church bells that morning when he'd awakened, and doesn't that mean all eternity has been waiting for those birds to rise up and putter, each on its appointed spot, each hopping about no more, no less than its allotted number of hops along the razor edge of rooftop, every second accounted for, poised, primed to happen, and must align itself ahead or behind the appearance of a flight of birds the dirt color of almost transparent shadows, four creatures gathering to touch down together on top of a whitish building with its meager, barred terraces, deeply recessed windows, tiny heads and breasts all he could see of the birds until they swoop off riding invisible ropes like mountain climbers rappelling, swiftly gone, and will another eternity pass or the same one pass once again before the birds, attuned to some simple fixed design, like seasons changing or clock hands recycling, alight again precisely as he'd glimpsed them alighting just an instant ago, except meanwhile gears and pulleys, streaming particles of light and bundles of light tearing each other apart or fumbling

129

under one another's clothes inside dark rooms of the apartment building across the way, have transformed in the twinkling of an eye, the 1, 2, 3, 4 birds and every other possible bird and each and every concrete block stacked, cemented together to form the structure atop which the birds jiggle a moment, all of that and the universes containing it crumbled to dust then nothing then starting over and starting to crumble again during an unfathomable interval between two iron links in the chain of being, the stroke of one moment connected to the next stroke and if he misses the next one where would he be then.

Walking Girl

Maria my walking girl. Walks and walks me with her brown, skinny legs I don't see but see boys and old men happy to see all the long, bare brown of when the city's hot and in her shorts or pretty short dresses she walks behind me walking my chair, its spinning wheels my legs I grip and shove to scoot maybe a slow inch this way or that when I sit home alone and get tired of being a broken, scared bug flipped over on its back, tired of just sitting still, still as a pile of sticks and stones dumped in the chair unless someone pushes or lifts me out from one place to another to eat or watch TV on the sofa or sleep or let my pee trickle or bowels empty or be cleaned.

Yesterday afternoon I dreamed it was night and dreamed I was Maria dreaming of being me, me lifting Maria in my soft, white arms, my brown sweet, baby Maria but almost big as me, big as my big hug like a fluffy warm white cloud all around her, Maria dry and safe in my arms rocking and cooing and dreaming of being me one day, me the long-legged walking girl walking perfect forever round and round the same dozen or so city blocks walking and daydreaming and in the dream every person equal to every other and they can switch back and forth changing places with ease so when you're tired of being one person you can be another without hurting anybody and nobody, nothing lost you're the one walking sometimes or the one pushed in a wheelchair or brown or white or tall or short on different days who cares, fat or thin, boy or girl just so we take turns and I can be the one once in a while who gets a call and laughs into a phone small enough to hold in the palm of my hand, *Hi. Howya doing. What's up. Hey, babycakes*, hearing words that change me suddenly like people change in my dream, me parking the chair in the shade and stepping away for a bit for privacy, O.K, but I'm happy Maria can watch someone's words bless me and sparkle me, my hard shiney hair, painted toes, tiny white teeth, dark eyes flashing, hip jutted out like young mothers with a cute baby asleep on it, and I giggle, dance a little salsa step and smile at her like, Maria, darling, don't go nowhere, child. Be right back to get you in a minute, my girl.

Genocide

The first time I watched him play he was so good I wanted to cry. He had it all. The body, mind, will. A big, black, bouncey kid everywhere at once on the hoop court. So good the game came to him. And all the other players knew, whether they liked the fact or not, knew if they wanted the game's shine a moment on the best they could bring when they played the game the way it should be played, they needed him. The best action starting up and swirling round him, choosing him, opening its heart to him each time he set foot on the asphalt court.

First time I saw him playing the court shrunk infinitesimally small then zoomed infinitely large, as small then large as the invisible Buddha head floating above it, the gaze of whose curled, hooded eye fixed on the game turns the play perfect because a Buddha could see it in no other fashion, though everything out there imperfect, yearning to be more, to be less, to be other than it is, all that sadness and incompleteness forgotten in the Buddha's smiling certainty this Universe and all the Universes containing it are moving along just fine, thank you, nothing out of place, everything present without the pain of birth or death, just give the boy the ball and get out of the way, the Buddha's golden gaze speaking palpable as a cityscape, a sunset or sunrise framing tacky, crooked backboards and poles on Homewood court the July day I first saw him play.

Like seeing myself out there playing perfectly. Or rather seeing for the first time the game played the way I'd always dreamed of playing it and seeing the one playing the game that perfect way didn't need to be me for my dream to come true and make me happy beyond words, so happy I understood instantly it couldn't last, wouldn't last, and tears began welling up behind my eyes, ready to mourn, to concede and despair since nothing this good ever stays this good long. I wanted to kill him. Grab that big nigger and put him on ice. Set him free so I wouldn't have to watch the pop or slide of him going down slowly, coming apart. Stash his ass somewhere safe. Somewhere nothing, no one could touch him with a corrupting touch. Me first.

Mercury

Same summer Tommy saw in *Jet* magazine a scary photo of a dead boy almost exactly his age, a dead boy whose face looked to him like a black bug somebody had squashed under their thumb, for a couple months of that same hot summer a brand new, spit-shined car and the large man who owned it the best things happening on Tommy's end of Copeland street where a few raggedy houses held the few coloreds who lived just down from the stores of Walnut street in Shadyside, Pittsburgh, Pa. Tommy couldn't get enough of the long, streamlined F-86 Sabre jet slick Merc or its twice man-sized owner, Big Jim, who gave colored folks something to talk about because he rode the trolley downtown each morning for two weeks and sat his huge behind, baseball bat across his knee, in the Duquesne Light company office until they came to Copeland and turned his electricity back on.

Get your tail in here, boy: his father's iceberg voice from the kitchen. Why didn't you come in the house when your mother called you last night.

Wasn't late, Daddy. Not hardly past eight o'clock.

Didn't ask you what the time was. Don't care what time of night or day, boy, when your mother tells you do something, you know you better do it. And quick.

She called me out the window. I wasn't nowhere, Daddy. Just sitting downstairs right across the street in Big Jim's car where Mom could see me.

Since when you grown enough to be sitting around at night in anybody's car.

Wasn't going nowhere, Daddy.

Then what you two doing in that damned car.

Nothing.

What he say to you.

Nothing, Daddy.

Well. I'll be talking to Mr. Big Jim soon's I get home from work tomorrow. Meanwhile, you're grounded, boy…Don't set foot out the door without you ask your mother. And if she say yes, don't you even think about going nowhere near that lard ass yellow man or his shit green car.

Three-toned green. Three colors a fad that summer. All kinds of brand new shiny rides in crazy color combinations dazzled the streets.

The Emmett Till photo story two-toned, white on black, a story about the old-timey terrible shit white men do to black boys down south. Not until a long time afterward would the boy begin to make any kind of precise sense of his deep fear, his father's deep anger, his own deep anger, his father's deep fear, the peacock cars, hate and terror and love, how in certain ways during that summer of 1955, all of it connects—including splashy, wobbly colors of a World Series in a Walnut Street store window playing on one of those new RCA TVs and the snowy, flip-flopping, black and white sets they'd keep watching for years down on his end of the block.

Work

Almost quiet back there. In the *bucket,* his word for the gleaming cylindrical container the truck hauled, the huge mixing bowl he and Eduardo remote controlled with buttons in the truck's cab. When it was working right, it could outperform a human hand. If you understood the buttons, the fingers of that big old steel fist inside the bucket could squeeze, shake, sort, chop, pick apart, shred, mix and blend its contents to a gritty pulp you pumped out at the dump, the entire job completed as a kind of invisible, mellow miracle once you got used to the stink and ignored the godawful grind and rumble of gears while the truck did its thing. The new ones will be absolutely soundproof, leak proof, they say, to protect driver and co-pilot in their high cab. Conchita far from new, that old ho Conchita his partner had named, she's the one he and Eduardo preferred. Old and reliably undependable in predictable ways, rather then those shiny, computerized, newer and newer models. Won't even need a driver soon. Technology the designers of the original fleet hadn't even dreamed of. Sun-powered. Quiet. No environmental damage. Perfect until they weren't. But then your troubles a 1000 times worse than dealing with the temperamental, old machines. You could fix this baby he rode regularly with Eduardo, their seniority giving them first pick each morning when crews mustered to chose a lover for the day's shift. Fix the bitch yourself out on the street and not lose a day's pay for missing in action, waiting to be towed. *Conchita* passing by some nights in his dreams, her bowl spinning, her hips bumping and grinding, drowning out the last screams of bad boys rounded-up, subdued, waiting to be packed in at each station along his daily route, bad kids of assorted colors, shapes, sizes so its not unfair, boys filling the bucket he empties, one load a day his contribution to peaceful streets, peaceful country, a promising life for boys like his sons who will ride up front one day, a good job, a family, a future.

Passing On

Why couldn't he choose. Blue suit or brown suit for the funeral. Throughout a long life, he'd endeavored to make sense of life, and now, almost overnight it seemed, the small bit of sense he'd struggled to grasp had turned to nonsense. Even the toys his grandkids played with mocked him, beeping, ringing, squealing, flashing products of a new dispensation he'd never fathom. Only pickly pride remained, pride in how he dressed, how he spoke the language, pride he hoped would allow him a dignified passage through final disappointments and fickleness. Unbending pride a barely disguised admission he's been defeated by that world he no longer pretends to understand and refuses to acknowledge except as brutal intervention, as disorder and intimidation constructed to humiliate him personally, pride wearing so thin he's desperate to recall skills his father might have taught him. Not the meager list of the skills themselves—not shining shoes, not tying a tie—but evidence of intimate exchange. Traces of the manner in which, through which, his father might have said, Here are some things I know, some things I am and I want to pass them on so you know them, too, and I hope they will serve you well. In other words he was aching to remember any occasion when or if his father had granted him permission to enter the unknown world his father inhabited a world that intersected only rarely with rooms shared with a wife and children. Who was his father. How was it possible to be the man his father was. A man attached and absolutely unattached. Where did he go when he left home. Did anything his father ever say suggest a son would be welcome in those other spaces that men occupied. Closure what he had learned from his father. The absolute abandonment of shutting down, disappearing. Cover-ups. Erasing all tracks. Eluding pursuit. Were those the skills. Teaching the shame of bearing an inexhaustible bag of useless tricks he knew better than to pass on.

Trouble

The man in the second place gives him a business card and directions to a third place but the third place isn't the right one either and he listens to a more complicated set of directions for reaching another place which will be the fourth place if he's remembering correctly what's happened already this morning with car trouble in a strange town, and various strangers who seem quite willing to be helpful even to the extent of drawing maps on scratch paper or repeating numerous times their instructions, listening intently, patiently to him as he explains his problem or the car's problem and he requires their patience because for some reason this morning he feels like he's speaking a second language, one he's not very good at, one you might as well say he's forgotten how to speak, it's that bad, he's reduced to a kind of baby talk, pidgin, grunt, point with fingers translation of words he's unsure of in his original language, whatever it is, if he owns one, and wonders if he possesses the car's papers, his papers, the papers for whatever lumpy, large thing it is he has no word for but suddenly recalls stuffing last night hurriedly into the car's trunk. Are papers tucked away, locked somewhere safely inside the car, papers explaining everything he can't say so that if or when he ever reaches the fourth place or fifth or however many places it's going to take, someone will understand him, believe him, fix the problem.

People of Color

Americans of all colors (even niggers) love sometimes to act like niggers. But nobody wants to be a nigger. Except maybe niggers (or perhaps not even niggers want to be niggers). Who knows. Ask one. How could we. Takes one to know one.

Dreaming Yellow Pianos

In the room crowded with yellow pianos no place to put my feet down I hover like all the silent music sealed under yellow covered keyboards and have not the slightest idea where this room might be or why I'm here unless it's simply to discover and celebrate my ignorance with not quite innocent questions no one, nothing exists to answer, though clearly I have power to give shape and color and substance to my thoughts or else how could I be in a room full of yellow pianos awaiting music without fingers, without a lid opening I'm expecting any moment now to awaken me.

Haiku

Toward the end of his life, a time he resided in France in self-imposed exile from America, the negro novelist Richard Wright chose the Japanese form *haiku*, an unrhymed poem of 3 lines, 17 syllables, as his principle means for speaking what burned inside him, the truths he needed to express each day till he died. Thousands of haiku and the thought of him working hour after hour, an ailing colored man from Mississippi, 52 years old, his international renown lynched by his fellow countryman, a brown man, trying again, one more time, to squeeze himself into or out of a tiny, arbitrary allotment of syllables dictated by a tradition conceived by dead strangers in a faraway land, Richard Wright in Paris hunched over a sheet of paper midwifing or executing himself within the walls of a prison others built without reference to dimensions required by a life that arched gigantically like his from almost slavery in the South to almost men on the moon, the idea of this warrior and hero falling upon his own sword on a battlefield rigged so he's doomed before he begins, the still multiplying and heartbreaking ironies of the man's last, quiet, solitary efforts—counting 1, 2, 3...5, 6, 7, up and back like a salsa dancer, or however, whatever you do, pacing, measuring your cage in order to do the thing he'd ended up doing, *haiku*, the thought makes me want to cry, but also sit back, shout in wonder.

Boy Soldier

I read about boy soldiers in Africa and wanted to be one. Not one kidnapped or orphaned or bullied or buggered or pulped in the wreckage of firefights and pogroms or gnashed in pointy yellow teeth of a beast who enjoys eating tender, smooth, brown bodies of boy soldiers, not one imprisoned, nor one unforgiven by his village or by himself for murder, rape, bloody kid games with deadly grown-up weapons, no, not one of those, nor one in whose nightmares a boy stalks or is stalked by a drooley monster with spinning lighthouse eyes he's become, none of the above but I find I like the idea of the worst that can happen to me going ahead and getting itself out of the way early, quickly, my world imploding or exploding because it's swallowed too much evil, spitting me out a.s.a.p., a survivor, squealing, wet, waves of incriminating memories a bloody spume I shake off like a dog vitus dancing to deflea itself, the worst passed, finished, done for all time, a chance to start again, seasoned veteran with many years left to play, years to become a better person, do my serious adult thing after I've been tried and absolved of childish sins—a parade someday, interviews, a pension perhaps—medals pinned to my bony breast.

Wolf Whistle

At first I think it's a mad boy let out of the attic or basement
for air an hour a day whistling at me from the rear of a long
yard, a demented boy unfamiliar with skin darker than his but
crazy enough not to be afraid, not to care, and whistles scorn, ra-
cial epithets, his shrill keening anger at being surprised, intruded
upon by a trespasser black as the devil or *ooh-la-la*, cutie pie,
what the fuck do we have here, sweetie, shrieked loud enough
for the whole neighborhood to enjoy in the long silence of Le
Moustoir at the eastern lip of Arradon on the Gulf of Morbihan
in the vicinity of Vannes in Brittany in France in Western Europe
in a Universe with ample space to incarcerate boys in Turkish-
looking, rusty cages crowned with minarets, hung on trees, two
of them, two cages umbrellaed by trees at the front of the long
yard belonging to a house on the corner of rue Saint Martin and
rue de la Touline I passed without seeing on daily walks to the
part tavern, part grocery store or morning strolls to the closest
sea or jogging five kilometers to Toulandac that opens like a tour-
ist's postcard dream when you turn a corner and coast parallel
to the coastline, Isle aux Moines, a gray lump framed in endless
blue distance by the long, slow smile of curve embracing double-
deck ferries, white sails, striped sails, a sailing school with pen-
nants flapping where kids try to learn to fly like fish and birds, a
convincing advertisement for the good life, a trick, achieved with
mirrors, even though happy, piping voices reach me there, all the
way up there on a road above Toulandac when I glide or pretend
to glide invisibly, effortlessly as the wind towards the fence-lined
path that cuts steep and straight down to the beach, to acres of

naked flesh, rocks and rocks and rocks, large as elephants, tiny as stinging gnats, families packed on weekends into this small, select space with stunning views almost to open sea, sea a bright lawn of water barely rippling as it laps the beach whose gently sloping sandy bottom remains visible underwater, many steps from shore, the footing awkwardly rocky through knee-high puddles of nodding algae, but soon smooth enough except for stones sharp as nails, blue, chilling water shallow for youngsters to wade far, far out, clear and calm, never a black triangle of fin crossing parallel to the horizon, no pain till you step out shivering, blue, slit open, the kids can play while you half watch, half doze, stupid in the sun, no need to ever get your feet wet or cold again, gashed again, your mad boy free a minute or two in the yard to wolf whistle or coo or cackle at Le Moustoir neighbors passing by, at children from the kindergarten across rue Saint Martin who break out early afternoons to car doors slamming then in again, their young mothers waiting naked and dazed as sunbathers or hiding in drabs colors of little donut cars jammed in the shade of trees adjacent to the house with a long yard on the corner where if I could ever get its attention, if I could ever master its language or the French language it might bi-lingually understand, I would teach one of the parrots or the other to be a mad boy again, not so mad he's locked in a cage but mad enough to whistle and hoot horribly obscene, scarey things at kids and their mothers, warning them about the bright razor sea you can smell from here and all the dead things in it, including pale skin of mothers burnt to ash, including children set out to play, set out nonchalantly like they're turned out to play in traffic on busy streets of this Universe shaped like a long yard from whose shadowy rear-end a hoarse, mocking, insane voice chops at me, cuts my legs from under me so I never make it to Toulandac one day, just kneel here, bleed here, outside the house's white stucco, chin high wall, begging forgiveness of a boy born mad and almost mute but he's picked up the gift of assaulting others with a few choice, nasty noises picked up from his Universe, on my knees imploring him to forgive me for blaming and cursing him because I saw for the first time two parrots staring, swaying, pecking gently at the bars of their rusted, oriental cages, two lynched birds I'd teach to warble *Emmett Till, Emmett Till* if I could, but they just sit there preening, ruffling their ratty feathers, each twin nailed to its perch, neither one making a sound in response to my coaxing, my artless imitations of them and I give up.

Stories

A man walking in the rain eating a banana. Where is he coming from. Where is he going. Why is he eating a banana. How hard is the rain falling. Where did he get the banana. What is the banana's name. How fast is the man walking. Does he mind the rain. What does he have on his mind. Who is asking all these questions. Who is supposed to answer them. Why. Does it matter. How many questions about a man walking in the rain eating a banana are there. Is the previous question one of them or is it another kind of question, not about the man or the walking or the rain. If not, what's it a question about. Does each question raise another question. If so, what's the point. If not, what will the final question be. Does the man know any of the answers. Does he enjoy bananas. Walking in the rain. Can the man feel the weight of eyes on him, the weight of questions. Why does the banana's bright yellow seem the only color, the last possible color remaining in a gray world with a gray scrim of rain turning everything grayer. I know question after question after question. The only answer I know is this: all the stories I could make from this man walking in the rain eating a banana would be sad, unless I'm behind a window with you looking out at him.

Bones

Those are my mother's bones, I said to him after he placed them white, puckered like coral on the desk, looking at me strangely as if to say, We're here to find bones, aren't we, and I've found some and brought them to you and you're looking at me like I've broken some deep rule, your eyes close to tearing up, an uneasy silence between us sealed in place with anger, the admonishing tone of your voice assaulting me for no reason I can imagine, accusing me of a crime though you've ordered me and pay me well to commit it. Bones. Dug up. Sifted from ancient rubble. God knows whose bones. Why shout, *Take them back. Take them away from here.* As if they could be returned. Replaced in their holes. As if sitting here flesh still clings to them, raw and unforgiving. Belonging to someone else. Please I beg you take them back into those empty hands of yours, huge hands dangling from a worker's long-muscled, hairy, bare arms, sweat and dust-streaked tendons and veins twisting like rope, like tributaries into a delta. Why are you standing there with a put-upon, abused expression forming around your mouth, eyes lowered that would be blank if you lifted them, naked and blank as bones exposed to your naked gaze when you scooped them in a sieve from the pyramid of sediment in which they'd been hidden, gingerly shook them to let sand trickle away, then laid them in a cloth and hurried here to my office for your reward.

My mother's bones. How could I expect you to know how many years I've been waiting to cry. To begin mourning a loss far too profound to face, too heavy to bear as long as I could find ways of not facing, not bearing. Hesitant, empty as your hands, reluctant as your hands to start over or go back and undo what's been done after you've been told it's wrong and too late you can't change anything, guilty of whatever there is to be guilty of, sins you never knew were sins and still don't, but ignorance no excuse, grants no remission, though you stand head bowed, open-mouthed, empty-handed, accused for no reason you understand. Guilty. The fair and unfairness of no consequence. Responsibility the wrong word. Always too late. Too fragile a protection. Like bones. Failed white bones pitted as dice, like dry bits of sponge on my desk.

Fly

A fly is something that enters your domestic relations through a window you carelessly leave open. No one else to blame but yourself, a fly symptom not cause of your problems, the fly a peripheral phenomenon, buzzing around your shit now and then, nothing personal, it's anonymous, almost unheard, almost invisible or perhaps so aggressive you go nuts trying to swat it or get lucky and *blat,* the monster's gone, you're free at last to continue carrying on your business relatively undisturbed or a fly may endure to celebrate your demise, the messy end of your affairs, its twitching hairy legs all up in your body cavities and you can't even scream or shoo it away, but so what, at that point who cares, you won't feel its whiskers, its knobby, blue-bulbed proboscis rooting, a fly just a fly, afterall, and you are what you are, buzz, buzz, gone, flying away.

Match

Jules and Rita were rivals in the office, and, therefore, hated each other. You'd often overhear, even when you didn't try, words like sexist, racist, pig, bitch, chauvinist, dike, punk in the conversations about the other each regularly engaged in with colleagues. So it came as a great surprise when eyewitnesses reported that Rita and Jules embraced, then kissed, a kiss hotter, it was said, than licks of fire driving them to the window ledge where they joined hands and leaped, falling like birds aflame the day two 767s toppled the Twin Towers.

"Now wait a damned minute. Like birds aflame and kisses hotter than fire. What the fuck are you talking about, you meathead. Obviously you weren't there," said the letter in response to the story's appearance.

Exchange

How come your stories always about bad stuff. Why don't you write a happy story. Write one makes people laugh.

Your advice absolutely right on, honeybun. And I will surely try. Just thinking about making people laugh tickles me inside. Now open up those big, pretty legs you're sitting on over there so I can jump in and spread the good news.

You're not being nice. I think you're poking fun at me.

No. No. I'm dead serious, lil darling. You're the one concocting a sad story now. A hurting story about boy meets girl, loves and loses her when she says no and the boy dies an unfulfilled dirty old man. Sounds like one of those sorry tales I used to tell before you showed me the light. C'mon now and drop them drawers, girl. Turn the boy on to some that sweet inspiration.

O.K. OK. If you insist. You're the writer, afterall. And these days, well, a girl's got to be prepared to part with a little poontang if she wants to get along. No big thing. Going along to get along. But I better warn you. I be stone HIV positive. Dead before two Christmases, the doctor said.

Whoa, girl. Why you got to start up another sad story. Thought you said you heard enough sad stories. Thought you said you wanted a happy story. Thought you wanted to laugh.

Who says I don't. Who says I won't. Better get it on, Mister authorman. We ain't got much time.